To Greta +

Much love !

—Jo

DIRTY DOCTORS

By John Fleer

ISBN: 978-0-9600687-0-8

Copyediting by Author One Stop, Inc. (www.AuthorOneStop.com)

Design and production by Joanne Shwed, Backspace Ink (www.backspaceink.com)

*A book has a life of its own, a fate of its own,
maybe a heaven or hell, for all I know.*

—Jorge Luis Borges

Everything in life is about sex, except sex, which is about power.

—Congressman Francis Underwood, *House of Cards*

Many friends and family members reviewed earlier versions of this book. The final product reflects their feedback and encouragement.

Thank you to Marika, Max, Juna, Alex, Jake, and Jason. Thank you to Elizabeth Ryan, Rich Gelman, Sara Harris, Gary Ware, Greta Sholachman, Mark Zaslav, Marty Williams, Carol Moertl, Linda Niemioja, Marcia Schuyler, Paul Raub, Jennifer Paige, and Steve and Marsha Rouch.

A few years ago, I met Pulitzer Prize-winning author Tom Parker as we shared a tiny jazz-club table. He generously offered to read my manuscript and offer his thoughts. A short course in writing fiction followed. Special thanks to him.

Randy Peyser (Author One Stop) and Joanne Shwed (Backspace Ink) have expertly guided the final stages. They have been terrific.

CONTENTS

JUSTICE

Anticipation: That's what life is mostly about. And relief. And regret. What's left? The measure of the man perhaps.

You are waiting, pacing, and waiting.

You wonder why you so often put yourself through this. It's the same thing you always wonder while you wait on a jury to return with its verdict.

It is truly painful but, of course, not physically. It is mental torture. You would love to employ any of your tried-and-true remedies for psychological distress. But alcohol, pot, and sex are off limits in superior court hallways. Years ago, you might have headed for a bathroom stall to snort some South American decongestant. But that is long behind you now. In any event, all that ever did in these situations was make you sweat and suffer more.

Twelve strangers are sitting in a windowless room and deciding your fate. Well, not really *your* fate but the fate of your client. In this case, your client is a dead man. Literally. You remind yourself that his fate is already decided. In fact, Dr. Lucas Golden's "fate" was to die suddenly of a heart attack at age 68 while reading a bedtime story to his three-year-old son.

The living person with a dog in this fight (besides you) is Dr. Golden's good-looking and youthful widow Laura. There is an insurance company in the mix as well. Dr. Golden's malpractice carrier pays your fees but would argue with Dr. Golden's estate attorneys over who pays what in the event of a negative jury verdict. If you prevail, you stand to gain further case assignments from the insurance company and Golden's heirs keep all their inheritance. You also have a crush on the widow and would definitely like to make her happy.

There is a stairwell in a quiet courthouse corner next to the custodian's closet. You nonchalantly open the metal door marked EXIT and peer up and down the stairs. You see no one. Better yet, you see no security camera. You head halfway up the steps, and then extract the single cigarette you carry for times like this. You officially stopped smoking 15 years ago. But you take a tobacco hit whenever you have a chance to surreptitiously do so in a stressful situation. Which means, of course, that you are still a smoker. You do not know the current legal sanctions for smoking in a public building. But they are probably somewhere between extended community service and chain gang.

Any kind of incident with the forces of authority would be very, very bad right now. You must not be exposed to the trial judge or the jury as a miscreant. But the anticipation of sweet smoke being sucked into your lungs is getting stronger by the moment. You calculate that you can easily get three to four (okay, maybe five) lungfuls, fling the butt down three flights, and escape the stairwell before any smoke detector does its thing. You have no way of assessing the odds that another person will enter your temporary sanctuary while you are committing your criminal act. But that is the risk all people on the wrong side of the law take as a matter of routine. It is routine for you as well.

You flick your lighter, light the Marlboro, inhale your five doses, scrunch the butt on the metal banister, and let it fall out of sight. The regret for your actions kicks in as you slink back into the hallway. Relief builds as no alarms are sounded. No one pays you any mind, and you resume pacing.

You have the acute realization that you have made some wrong turns. Not just this past minute. Pretty much all of your 49 years on the planet. You always have a realization during these waits: Once upon a time, you were going to pursue training as a neuropsychologist; then, for some vague reason, you instead went to law school and became an attorney. Twenty-two years now, despite the fact that you don't much like attorneys and despise the "justice system," which is anything but. It exists for and perpetuates the interests of the haves—not the have-nots.

You married your high school sweetheart. Three divorces later, you got the message that you may not be cut out for married life. You may not be cut out for the legal profession either. You have bounced around quite a bit, never finding a comfortable long-term position in the legal world.

You'd rather not wear a suit and tie to work. But that's part of the job. You wouldn't mind starting over. Unfortunately, you make just enough money to support kids, ex-wives, and a number of your own expensive habits. You doubt that you could manage these things in a new job. Oh, well. You have your health (as they say). God knows why.

You try to refocus. The jury has been in deliberations for only three hours. Not long enough for you to start serious worrying. Jurors usually take at least enough time to get the free lunch, even if they have no doubt about the verdict. They also want to avoid the appearance of a rush to judgment. In your opinion, the worst thing about the O.J. Simpson trial in 1995 was that it made future jurors cautious about quick decisions. The media, which had milked O.J.'s trial around the clock, week after week, was greatly dismayed when the jury took about five minutes to make its decision. The jury members took all kinds of abuse from commentators for not sustaining the drama. Nowadays, jurors try to avoid criticism for not being careful and thoughtful enough. They stretch things out.

You, on the other hand, love quick decisions. They save you from all this fruitless self-analysis. As far as you are aware, no one has ever empirically established that a long debate among 12 people who review evidence and law results in a better decision than a bunch of folks simply giving thumbs up (or down) at the conclusion of a contest. (Yay, Rome!)

Thinking of Rome, you are wearing your best (and only) Italian suit. Most of your lawyer clothes are off the rack. You seek out two-for-one sales. You try to look prosperous, precarious as your real-world financial status is. Closing arguments require sartorial kicking out the jams. Look like a winner — maybe you will be. Lawyers adopt a strange mindset when the curtain is up and the pageant plays. Every detail becomes a topic for contemplation, reflection, and regret. As the end of trial draws near, you think not only of everything you have yet to do but everything you've already done. It is Second-Guess City. You are watching the play, directing the play, and criticizing the play. It's a play in which none of the actors want to perform. None of the audience wants to watch. Another asshole directs a parallel play in competition with you. You seek contrary outcomes from the same set of facts. Which one of you will succeed at exerting your will? Was that a hint of a smile yesterday from Juror #11? Did #4 frown at you?

You once had a female juror who tracked you down after trial in which you and your client had prevailed. She asked you to lunch. You thought she would give you some useful feedback. She gave you more than that. There is no ethical prohibition from having sex with former jurors. But you knew that she was having a liaison with an actor (you!) upon whom she projected qualities that you very much doubted. She said that she had fallen for your nervous habit of aggressively clicking your ballpoint pen whenever a witness was being a jerk. She was impressed by your command of the medical records and your heartfelt arguments. She wanted to make plans for future dates. She wanted you to meet her family. When you declined to commit, she angrily revealed that she had initially cast her vote for the plaintiff and now regretted having been pressured by the majority to let your "scumbag client" off the hook. She now saw that you were the kind of man who "leads women on." You departed, silently vowing to control your pen-clicking and to not return calls from former jurors. What happens in the courtroom needs to stay in the courtroom.

The moral, of which you now remind yourself, is that you never know what a juror is thinking. Twelve people you don't know are making a decision that is likely to be inexplicable. You ponder man's essentially hopeless quest for meaning in a random universe.

You continue to pace the halls. Periodically you circle back to your courtroom to see if there are any signs of activity. The shrewish court clerk shuffles paper, and the sleepy bailiff scratches himself. You might as well be waiting for Godot.

Whatever the final result, you think that you have outdone yourself on this trial. Your dead client had been sued by his former psychiatric patient Lois Sutcliffe. She claimed that, during the course of 15 years of therapy, Dr. Golden had systematically seduced her, engaged in a long-term sexual relationship with her, and undermined her mental health, keeping her in a perpetual state of dependence.

Ms. Sutcliffe is represented by a well-known and successful plaintiffs' attorney: Mal Schiff. You despise Schiff. He is fat, ugly, obnoxious, and unfortunately very smart. He is also willing to do anything to win his cases. This is the second time you have been in trial against him. In the previous trial, he gave a lengthy closing argument in which he fell to the floor in tears as he lamented the damage done to his female client by yours— an elderly, goofball physician who had gratuitously copped a feel. Schiff shamelessly sprawled across the wooden floor. Water really did come out of his eyes. You had to admire that. You ponder your odd career niche.

You have represented dead people before. There are some good things about doing so. Living clients need their hands held and need to be assured that things will work out okay. They need to be told what to wear to court. There are a thousand ways they can screw up trial by what they do or say. Dead clients, on the other hand, don't need "strategy sessions." They don't call at night with anxious concerns. You don't have to take them to lunch. They don't give stupid answers on cross-examination by the opposition counsel.

Most importantly right now, you are not being interrupted in your solitary pacing and obsessing. You start to replay the two weeks of trial in your mind. There are many things that you might have done differently. Fortunately, you kept the jury from learning one very bad fact about Dr. Golden. You had managed a dicey situation. You can't decide whether you feel good about your skillful advocacy or bad about being a typical dickhead, sneaky lawyer. A little of each, you guess. Most of all, you are pleased that your basic trial strategy was carried off.

With the testimony of multiple experts and therapists who had worked with Ms. Sutcliffe over the years, you painted a compelling (you think) picture of Ms. Sutcliffe as a borderline personality. Your experts testified that people with such a disorder initially idealize those who help them but ultimately come to hate them for insufficiently doing so. A caregiver may be seen as a savior, and then despised as a monster. This shift is triggered by feelings of abandonment. Dr. Golden had "abandoned" Lois Sutcliffe when he died. That was why this meritless lawsuit had been filed — or so you had argued. Another way to put it was that you had attacked Ms. Sutcliffe's credibility on the basis of her mental illness. You wonder if perhaps that turned off or offended the jury. Maybe they think you are a bum for smearing an abused woman. You want to find out. You want the jury to finish its damn job!

The bailiff is approaching from down the hall. Is he gesturing for you? Yes!

"The foreperson gave me a note for the judge. He wants to see counsel in his chambers."

This is not particularly good news. It is not unusual for the jury to write questions during deliberations. But it is irritating to trial attorneys. The questions are not often easily answered and are typically discussed and argued at length before the judge sends back a response. It is impossible to resist overinterpretation of the question because it is the only glimpse you have of what the jury might be thinking. In any event, it means that the waiting will continue. Sweat threatens to ruin your Egyptian cotton shirt.

You and Schiff are ushered into the judge's chambers. If this judge has a personality, he has done a good job of hiding it for two weeks. He has a quintessential poker face.

Somberly, he intones, "The jury has a question."

You *know* that!

"It also has a verdict," he concludes.

That is weird.

"The question is this: Will Ms. Sutcliffe be able to learn our home addresses and telephone numbers, or can the court keep them confidential?"

Schiff looks blank for a few beats. Then his eyes bulge in anger. You figured it out quickly. What an intelligent group of jurors! They must have totally bought what you were selling. They want nothing to do with crazy Lois!

"I never doubted them," you lie to yourself.

You have spent a lot of time with liars this past year. Maybe you have picked up some bad habits.

A YEAR AGO

"You're late! Again!"

"Jesus, Kate. If I wanted to start the day being yelled at for my lax personal habits, I'd have stayed married."

"Excuse me for worrying that Dr. Thomas has been waiting in the conference room for half an hour. He might actually be a paying client. And the California Physicians' Trust (CPT) has called with a possible case assignment, which I thought you cared about since you have been schmoozing their claims people for months, begging for work. And, according to Lawrence, the first bill collector of the day has already called."

"Good comeback. I'll see Dr. Thomas first. Do I have a tie around here somewhere?"

You are just another middle-aged white guy with a solo law practice. Dime a dozen. You previously worked in law firms big and small. There seems to be some kind of problem in working well with others. You recall such a comment being made on your grade school report card. You need to improve your attitude and your wardrobe. You need a haircut.

Your office is on the ground floor of a converted Victorian building located in a somewhat seedy Oakland neighborhood. You have clients and try cases throughout the San Francisco Bay Area. Oakland is conveniently located in the middle of those venues, and the rents are cheaper than in the city across the bridge. The Victorian building is owned by an old Chinese couple. They look more worn and torn every time you see them. The building needs an upgrade too. It wouldn't hurt to have the yard mowed or the vines trimmed. Fortunately, the rent is commensurate with indifferent maintenance in a crappy locale.

You employ a sassy paralegal. Kate is mid-30s, smart as the proverbial whip, and fashionable in a way that you remotely appreciate. She has short,

15

spiky black hair and a good figure. She is sometimes a definite pain in the ass. But you appreciate that as well. You know that you do your best work when someone keeps you on your toes. You sometimes sort of flirt with each other. Neither seems interested in taking it further. You are aware that, at this point in your life, any woman willing to risk emotional entanglement with you would have extremely poor judgment. Kate does not suffer from that.

Your other employee is Lawrence, a competent and corpulent secretary. You never think of him as having any age. He is meticulous but refrains from commenting on your disorganization and slovenly habits. He does, however, look at you like you are a retard. He also rolls his eyes when you say words like "retard."

When in a positive state of mind, you think of your legal career as having evolved to a simple and efficient state. More often, you recognize that you are progressively hanging by a thinner and thinner thread. The preacher Jonathan Edwards referred to that thread as hanging with "the flames of divine wrath flashing about it." God can cut it when he pleases. A humanities-rich education has its insecure downside.

You have a reputation with other attorneys as a guy who represents doctors with "delicate problems." Translation: You defend doctors who get in trouble for sexual misbehavior, drugs, alcohol, and psychiatric disorders. You have and always have had plenty of work. You also are pretty good at it. But you don't always send bills for your services, you don't always get paid when you do, and you suck at running a business. You know that, if you just "got it together," you could take care of ex-wives, children, employees, and bill collectors — not to mention the tax authorities. Getting it together is perpetually elusive, even if occasionally in sight on the horizon.

"One foot in front of the other," you tell yourself.

Let's start with the new guy in the conference room.

"Kate, what's the story with Dr. Thomas?"

"Marin County psychologist in private practice. He is being sued for sexual misconduct with a client. I don't have any information yet on his financial status. Let's hope he turns out to be a *paying* customer."

"Hope springs eternal."

"I'm serious. Have you seen the accounts receivable report for the past two months?"

"I love it when you go all CPA on me."

Kate drops her voice an octave. "There are times when I question the unusual business niche that you've been nurturing. Maybe you should give some consideration to the fact that no other lawyers seem to be lining up to do this kind of work. I have my own job security to worry about too."

"We are pretty busy," you lamely reply.

"Busy working for people who can't or won't pay doesn't count!"

Man, she is getting worked up. You decide to take diversionary measures.

"You can't make an omelet without breaking a few eggs!"

"That has nothing to do with what I am talking about!"

"I know. But you can't."

"Can't what?"

"Make omelets without egg-breaking. I've tried. It was a mess and inedible."

"I can't believe I am working for someone who talks like that!"

"It *is* different, isn't it?"

Lawrence pokes his head in the doorway, arches his eyes, and points (pointedly) to his fat, freckled wrist as if he were wearing a watch. You march into the conference room. Kate follows.

Dr. Thomas is another mid-40s white guy. Unlike you, he looks energetic and fit. He also looks worried. You know lots of yuppie professionals like him. He undoubtedly is a regular at the gym (probably has a long-time personal trainer), believes himself "spiritual" because he once went to a weekend meditation retreat, and makes a point of staring in your eyes when he talks to convey how earnest he is. Or maybe he is a depraved, methamphetamine junkie who somehow has kept his teeth in really good condition. No, you'll bet on option one.

You exchange introductions and some small talk concerning the weather, the traffic today, and the office artwork. The doctor gets credit for accurately recognizing the framed Quicksilver Messenger Service poster. Finally, he gets around to the reason for the journey to Oakland and to you.

"I've been sued. I still can't believe it! Loren Patagorkis, my former patient, claims that I had sex with her. It's a lie! I asked around, and several people told me that you were the person I should retain to represent me."

You ask for the complaint and scan it.

Meanwhile, Kate cuts in. "Do you have professional liability insurance?"

"Never dreamed I would need it," says (the now slightly less energetic) Dr. Thomas.

Kate looks at you wearily.

You do your economics lecture: "The defense of a case like this is always expensive. It might be cheaper to just pay off the plaintiff and move on with life. The attorney who filed this complaint on behalf of Ms. Patagorkis is represented by one of the best plaintiffs' attorneys in California. We have had plenty of experience with Mr. Lewis. He is not cheap either. It is going to take a lot to get him off your back. My rate is $300 an hour, and I require," I say while looking at Kate, "a $10,000 retainer."

Kate returns your look with something resembling admiration. You have seen that look on women's faces before. It both scares and excites.

You continue. "Of course, we will need to hear all the details from you. But you have already said the most important thing: The complaint is false. If so, I can assure you that Kate and I will do everything in our power to defend and exonerate you."

You pull your fee agreement out of a slick, blue folder and lay it before Dr. Thomas.

"Review this, Doctor. Take as long as you need. If it meets with your approval and you have your checkbook handy, just date and sign here, write out the check, and we are in business." You fear that deep down you have the heart and soul of a used-car salesman.

You and Kate exit the room, leaving Dr. Thomas to the cold reality of his predicament.

Kate says, "You acted like a responsible business owner in there!"

You do the Dr. Thomas stare into her eyes. "A rolling stone gathers no moss, grasshopper."

"You are an idiot," she says as she holds your stare for a second longer than expected.

You continue to flex your business acumen. "Lawrence, stand by for a bank run."

You return to the conference room where Dr. Thomas hands you the contract and check. You slickly sidle to the door and toss the papers to Lawrence, who is crouched nearby.

"Well, Doctor. Tell us about Loren Patagorkis."

"I'll try not to be disrespectful. But I think she must be a psychopath."

You put on your most thoughtful expression and offer, "Did you write that down anywhere before she filed a lawsuit against you?"

Dr. Thomas has a vacant look in his eyes.

"No, I thought not," you confide. "Let's hear the facts."

"Loren is 32 years old. She came to see me because she was in a rut. She was dissatisfied with life. She worked as a paralegal at a large San Francisco law firm. She had been an excellent student in high school and college. She decided to get out into the real world, rather than pursue graduate studies. She landed a well-paying job with the law firm and shared an apartment in Mill Valley with a female coworker. She dabbled in the singles scene but came to find the bars and clubs uninteresting. She had brief, unsatisfactory relationships with men. She was obviously suffering from depression."

"Join the club," you think.

Dr. Thomas continues. "I encouraged her to identify the kind of life she wanted for herself and map out the steps to achieve it."

You wonder if people really think this way about plotting out their lives and the lives of others. Apparently, they do.

"Loren did not want to return to school," Dr. Thomas says, "but she did want another kind of job. I referred her for vocational testing, which revealed an aptitude in sales. Loren agreed that a job with more human contact would be to her liking. I offered my office computer to work on her resume and do some job hunting after our therapy sessions. We drafted cover letters to prospective employers. Sometimes she would stay an hour or so after our formal sessions while I caught up on paperwork.

"One day, she called to say that she was stranded with a flat tire and would not be able to make her appointment. I got her location and drove to her. I helped her change her tire, and we made it back to the office for a short session. I was trying to show her by example how one could deal with an adverse situation and feel reinforced for having conquered it.

"Because Loren worked during the day, I usually reserved the last appointment for her. We typically exchanged hugs before leaving but nothing more. One day, she didn't show up. She did not return my telephone calls. A month later, I was served with this lawsuit. I tell you, it's just not true. I will take a lie detector. Anything!"

By now, the doctor's façade of control, calm, and confidence has deteriorated to a puddle of self-pity. He is tearful and distraught. You and Kate try to discourage him more. You dispel any illusion of technological assistance.

"I hear you, Doc. Unfortunately, lie-detector tests are not admissible in court. There is controversy about whether they are foolproof. Some people pass one lie-detector test and flunk another. For better or worse, we have juries."

Kate chimes in. "If I may, I have some concerns about what you have told us. Researchers have studied factors associated with psychotherapist-patient sex. They have identified a 'slippery slope' of therapist behaviors, which correlate with the therapist and the patient developing a sexual relationship. Some of what you have said are textbook examples, allowing the patient special privileges or accommodations, expanding the time for therapy sessions, out-of-the-office contacts, arranging sessions at the end of the day, and physical, even if seemingly innocuous, contacts, like those little hugs."

You feel the need to tone down the onslaught. "Well, that's just a lot of stuff lawyers like to throw against the wall. They don't prove misconduct."

"Loren's attorney knows all about how to throw it," Kate rejoins.

You sit silently for a long moment. You note the moisture on the doctor's upper lip. You note Kate's fiery eyes. You take special note that you and your paralegal seem to be playing good cop/bad cop with a client who just paid you ten grand.

You assume your best professorial tone. "Here is the plan. We answer the complaint and deny these spurious allegations. We learn all we can about Loren's background. We take her deposition and hear the details of her story and assess her potential jury appeal. We gain an understanding of who she is and what has led her to make this false claim. Money is always a reason. But it is never the only reason for someone to lie like this."

You have stroked Dr. Thomas and regained his confidence. Listen to yourself! You just made something very difficult sound easy. You wink at Kate.

She mopes. She's not done with Dr. Thomas. "Do you have any distinctive marks or features that only someone who was physically intimate with you would identify?"

"What?"

You assist. "Any scars on your naughty bits?" You need to stop channeling Monty Python.

"What?"

You rephrase. "Is there anything noteworthy about your private parts? Marks? Physical anomalies? Moles? Remarkable proportions?"

"Actually, there is something. My pubic hair has turned prematurely gray. It's been like that for years."

"Is there a third party who could verify that?" you ask.

"I'll show you."

"No, thanks. We'll leave that for Lawrence. He gets so few perks in his job. Can anyone testify that you had a prematurely gray crotch during the time you treated Ms. Patagorkis?"

"I have an ex-wife. She could."

Kate again. "Do you have any staff? Is there anyone who saw you and Ms. Patagorkis together?"

"No one I can think of."

"Written communications between you two? Any phone messages? Letters? Cards?"

"No, no, and no."

"What about your treatment records?" Kate inquires.

"I'm not much of a recordkeeper."

"So … you have no records?"

"I have an intake sheet and dates of service. I don't keep much else in the way of records. It takes up too much time. I put everything I have into my client."

You and Kate exchange grimaces as you make a mental note to eliminate that phrase from the doctor's repertoire.

LATER THAT DAY

You return the phone call from the CPT. It is a large insurance company, which insures thousands of doctors. Some of them are your kind of people — in trouble for screwing patients, doing drugs or alcohol to excess, being crazy, or all of the above. Once in a while, some doctors are falsely accused of these things. These are your favorite cases. You also know how to relate to those who truly have stepped over the line or snorted them to excess. Some of the "guilty" need your help to make the best deal they can. Some need your help to face the inevitable damage to their careers. Some need your help to dodge the consequences. You are open to all options.

The CPT has never worked with you before. But you have been selling yourself diligently. In the insurance-defense world, that means you have kissed a lot of ass, bought a lot of lunches, and generally behaved as though insurance-claims people are somewhat smarter and interesting than they are. You have not gone to the lengths of some of your peers. You haven't sent cases of Scotch or purchased trips to Hawaii for claims adjustors. You haven't golfed, for Christ's sake. Still, it's only a matter of degree. All insurance-defense attorneys are feeding at the same troughs. Some just pay for better seats.

The rationale for participating in this humiliating grovel is that insurance companies have the cases. They pay lower rates, audit more, and are arrogant in their demands. But they pay more or less on time and can provide the security of continued streams of work. Many law firms have survived and prospered for years on the strength of two or three good insurance-company clients.

So, you are on the phone, perky as hell. "How can I help you today, Ms. Zimmerman?"

Ms. Zimmerman has an "unusual" case that calls for some "delicate" client handling. You love euphemisms. Ms. Z. is speaking your language. Someone has undoubtedly been accused of something sordid and is not being overly cooperative with the insurer. This is exactly what you need to prove yourself.

The upshot is that a psychiatrist is being accused of a long-term sexual relationship with his female client. The psychiatrist is dead. His estate is potentially liable for damages. But the CPT is potentially on the hook as well. The doctor's estate is represented by a very demanding attorney. The main beneficiary of the estate is the doctor's widow, who has not been easy for the insurance representative to contact or interview. The plaintiff is represented by an attorney with a big reputation, who has already made a $3 million settlement demand. That amount, not coincidentally, is the coverage limit of the doctor's CPT policy. The CPT can claim that it does not have to pay for physician-patient sex (excluded by the policy language as an "intentional act"). But it still has an obligation to provide defense counsel. The estate attorney requested that the CPT hire you after having asked some malpractice attorneys for their recommendations. Your name had been mentioned more than once. For the moment, everyone would like to be cooperative on the defense side. You are being invited to herd the cats. Cool.

You place a call to the attorney representing the estate of Lucas Golden, MD. A meeting with the widow Golden is arranged. The attorney talks of the "family's interests," "Dr. Golden's trust holdings," and the "tax ramifications of the insurance-coverage issues." You don't understand that much of what he is saying. But it smells like big money to you. You are right.

MEETING LAURA

The widow Golden lives in Atherton, a San Jose suburb one step above affluent. Laura Golden receives you in her living room, and the family attorney is seated at her side. Laura is lovely. "Fragile" is the word that comes to mind. She is a slender 5'4", with light-brown hair and aquiline features. Her cornflower-blue eyes warrant the overused adjective "piercing." You notice her hands. They are fidgeting and active, though she otherwise seems calm. Her exaggeratedly large diamond wedding ring threatens to disrupt the otherwise perfect symmetry of her appearance.

Elliot French is the "family attorney." You have never met an attorney named Elliot who did not have a stick up his ass. This one is impeccable.

A study in pearl gray —suit, shirt, tie, socks, and shoes. Where does someone buy pearl-gray wingtips? His specialty is estates and trusts. He is present to "facilitate" your meeting with Mrs. Golden and to advise you of your "primary responsibility" to the Golden estate, despite the fact that your fees will be paid by the insurance company. He talks down to you as if you were serving him cocktails at his gentlemen's club. His face reminds you of an overripe prune. You thank him for the clarification. Dickwad!

Lucas Golden, MD, was, by Laura's account, a kind and caring psychiatrist. If he had any fault, it was his unwillingness to terminate treatment with demanding and difficult patients. He was steady and steadfast in his devotion to their welfare. He answered phone calls from patients at any time, day or night. The most frequent intrusive caller was a female patient, known to Laura only as "Lois." When she called, Lucas would say her name and then retreat to his study or other private area to talk, sometimes for as much as an hour.

When Laura once complained of these interruptions, Lucas sighed and said, "Poor girl has no one else to help her through her difficult life. I have tried to transfer her to other therapists. It never works out."

As much as she hated the calls, Laura also admired her husband's patience and essential goodness. In fact, by Laura's account, Lucas Golden was pretty much a saint. He financially supported his first wife, and he maintained close relationships with his two older sons. He was a loving husband to Laura and had agreed to surgically reverse his vasectomy so that Laura could attain her goal of giving birth. He was devoted to little David. Lucas was respected by his professional peers. The heart attack had come without warning. But Dr. Golden had left his financial affairs in order and was well insured. There is no doubt that Laura and David will be secure. So, too, the first wife's alimony and college educations of the older sons will not be threatened. The oldest son Adam is currently in medical school and is a frequent visitor as big brother to David. He is also quite emotionally supportive to Laura. You wonder a little about that. You ultimately dismiss your sick-dog imagination.

You are not particularly attracted to helpless or weak women. But there is something about Laura Golden's vulnerability and lack of affectation that you find charming. She is putting herself "in your hands." You know that is not meant literally. But you enjoy the image.

Before you leave, Adam Golden shows up. He is a rakish young man, bearing the confidence of upper-class home and school. Nevertheless, you like him immediately. He is tall and lean with dark, wavy hair. He has an easy smile and manner. He would be good at selling stuff door to door, if anyone still did that kind of thing.

"My dad had his faults. But he loved his family, and he loved his work. I can only hope to someday be half as good of a father. I really appreciate your help in protecting his good name. That is far more important to me than the potential financial losses of this lawsuit. I will do anything I can to help."

Adam tells you about phone calls that family members received after Lucas's death. The calls came from a woman who identified herself as "Lois Sutcliffe, Dr. Golden's patient." She incessantly harassed Adam, his mother, his brother, and Laura with requests for information about the funeral and memorial. They all tried to put her off politely but ultimately had to bluntly tell her to leave them alone. Adam believes that a woman matching Lois's description had been keeping the house under surveillance at times. There have been no sightings since the lawsuit was filed.

Adam is finishing his third year of medical school. He is planning to become an internist. You all agree that he will be your primary contact with the family as needed. He is friendly to Laura but not overly familiar. His eyes light up when he mentions his half-brother David.

You are often at your most suspicious when your client or the facts of your new case sound so appealing. Dr. Golden must have had some warts, no? The widow Golden and her adult stepson may be keeping something from you. But they sure are attractive, nice rich folks. For now, you decide to take the path of least resistance. No probing questions. No outward expressions of doubt. You are looking forward to being of service and generating healthy billable hours.

FAREWELL JUDGE G.

The thrill of two new cases fades as the prospect of the work involved sets in. You are not a natural-born grinder. You are, by nature, an indolent slacker. But you are a creative, indolent slacker, and you enjoy the competitive nature of your business. There is a great deal of litigation grunt work to be accomplished to properly defend your new clients. It will get done — hopefully by substantial delegation to Kate — but you will (sooner or later) do your share.

Meanwhile, you have your personal and social obligations to attend to. There are not too many. Over the years, you have become more and more isolated, partly by choice and partly as a consequence of marital and law-firm dissolutions. You have a rare professional/social event this evening: a retirement party for a judge. You have known the Honorable Simpson Gilbert since you started your practice. He was old even then, and many attorneys think his retirement is long overdue. He is known for not suffering fools gladly. For some reason, he has pretty much always suffered you. You do not get invited to many of these types of events. You RSVPed out of curiosity and a little bit of pride that the judge apparently put you on the list.

The initial time that you appeared in Simpson Gilbert's court — and every time thereafter — you wondered if the judge's parents realized that they were bestowing a last name to a kid whose last name was a first one. Parents can be cruel, or odd, or clueless. Occasionally, you wonder how your children would describe your parenting. Probably with all three of those adjectives.

The party is being held, after hours, in the rotunda of City Hall. You present your engraved invitation to a tuxedoed doorman. You hope his clothing is not a reflection of the expected attire. No, fortunately the other attendees are wearing standard-issue lawyer work clothing: suits and ties for the men; suits (pants or a skirt) and tie substitutes or conservative necklaces for the women. You enter the vast space with its stained-glass ceiling. The partygoers are herded into a large circle framed by serving tables and bars. There are streamers, balloons, and a banner that reads, "We Love You, Judge G." It reminds you a bit of a Chucky E. Cheese's birthday party. You glance around to see if there is one of those inflatable jumping pits full of brightly colored plastic balls. That would be cool. But no.

You recognize many in the crowd. You are happy to see some of the familiar faces and less pleased to see others. Judges, lawyers, politicians. Bartenders and roaming servers in crisp, white shirts and black bowties. You spy an old nemesis heading your way. You feign glaucoma and veer sharply toward the nearest alcohol-dispensing station. You are relatively confident that you will find some of your friends in that vicinity.

"What a surprise to see you here!" exclaims Pearl Harris, your favorite transgender African American attorney. Pearl seemingly gets invited to everything in town. The hosts cover so many politically correct bases by inviting her. Notwithstanding that, Pearl is always on top of her game and knows the latest scandal. You and Pearl are just getting started with a combination of putdowns and gossip.

You are interrupted by an earnest competitor, Ronnie Cake. He also represents healthcare providers. But he behaves much better than you. It's not that you dislike him. You do not understand how his good manners, forced affability, and average intelligence combine to make him so financially successful. Ronnie presides over a thriving insurance-defense practice to which he always seems to be adding new associate attorneys.

He once asked if you were interested in working for his firm as a contract trial attorney to handle his "overflow." The resulting fees would be split 50-50. You were not that desperate (at least that day), so you pretended to be flattered but declined the offer. He is one of those people who profess a desire to "keep in touch." And here he is.

Ronnie has two judges in tow and starts making introductions. You are already well acquainted with Judge Beverly DeSantos. You have twice had the displeasure of trying cases in her department. She is crass and pigheaded. She has a porcine body type as well. It looks as though her chin is shining with grease. Maybe your harsh opinions of her countenance are somewhat influenced by the fact that she has so decidedly found against you and your clients. You are not at all above holding a grudge. You have not yet had your host-paid beverage or any of the hors d'oeuvres. You are peckish. This is a recipe for mild disaster.

Cell phones have been removed from pockets and handbags. Partygoers are taking photos of each other. This seems to correlate to lapses in conversation. ("I can't think of anything else to say to this moron, so let's take some pictures!") Ronnie asks Judge DeSantos to pose with you for a shot.

"I'm not going to have my picture taken with him," objects the Judge. "It would be like Michael Phelps being photographed with a bong!"

Laughter all around. You have just been analogized to a device for smoking pot.

"I don't want to pose with her either. It would make me appear malnourished." Not the subtlest jibe you have ever uttered. Judges, who are accustomed to dishing it out, are decidedly unaccustomed to taking it. There is a very loud silence. People are looking at their shoes.

Finally, a slim, young female server, carrying a platter of the world's tiniest ahi-topped crackers, pipes up. "Touché!"

There are chuckles. DeSantos turns her (ample) backside away from you. You stand your ground, waiting for some wine. The conversations start up again, though not the cell-phone photo shoots. You sense that you have just descended another few notches in the hierarchy of the "people who matter." You now have but two goals: to say "so long" to Judge Gilbert and to find and thank the perceptive young ahi server.

You understand that one of your worst traits is that, the more you understand how the world works, the less you tolerate it. Surely, maturity dictates an opposite reaction. The "maturity" thing has been a brittle bone of contention in every relationship you have had in the last 20 years or so. You frequently fail to anticipate the long-term consequences of your behavior (or so some women who knew you well have said).

But why should you accept the perpetuation of gross stupidity and injustice, even if it makes the world turn? Why go along to get along? Take tonight's little scene. Judges do not get honest feedback. Lawyers and litigants kiss up to them as a matter of course. Every day. Their staff employees are exceptionally deferential. The judge is addressed as "Your Honor" 100 times a day. In private, their associates laugh (excessively) at their jokes and praise their wisdom. You know that these bench sitters are appointed to the task for reasons that often have little to do with their exceptional intellect and personal qualities. But you all collude, for your own interests, to suggest otherwise. A black robe does not a wise or good person make. It is not a big mystery as to why they believe in the distorted praise and admiration. You wouldn't mind some of that yourself, although you would never pass the background check that would allow you to be considered for the job.

In your immature view, you refuse to be overly effusive to the judiciary when outside a courtroom. In court, you have the ability to kiss ass with the best of them. But, more often, your facial expressions and tone of voice give away disbelief and disapproval. The long-term consequence is that you rarely get invited to a power lunch in this town.

There was a different vibe between Judge Gilbert and you. He never seemed overly impressed with any lawyer or with himself. He treated everyone — plaintiffs, defendants, their counsel, jurors, court employees, and judge colleagues — the same: crotchety and direct. He was intimidating because he didn't like obsequious bullshit. You felt at home, if not at ease, in his courtroom. You locate Judge Gilbert, surrounded three deep by well-wishers. There is no way you will wait for that crowd to disperse. You order a double martini from the bar and ask for the loan of a serving tray.

"Excuse me. Coming through! Special delivery for Judge Gilbert!" You slice through the crowd and deposit the cocktail into the gnarled hands of the judge.

"I always knew that you were good for something," he snarls.

"I will miss you, you old rascal," you reply. You man hug each other. You walk off. Once again, you seem to have had the effect of momentarily silencing the crowd.

The young ahi woman is reloading her platter at the outskirts of the room. As you approach, you have several rapid realizations. She is really young. She is overworked. Going out of your way to talk to her at this party is not exactly going to help her public image. You do not want to bother her, despite whatever depraved fantasies you might have started developing. Just as you redirect for the exit, your eyes meet. You wave. She smiles. *Nice.* It takes so little to please a middle-aged man.

MALTESE FALCON

You come home and put on a DVD of your favorite movie, *The Maltese Falcon*. You watch it at least once a year. You believe that you understand the real meaning of this film. Beneath the wild plot of a quest for the precious falcon statuette, the murders, and the outrageous characters who manipulate and betray each other, there is a deeper concern running throughout. Sam Spade (played by Humphrey Bogart) struggles to figure out women.

Sam is a bachelor. But it is obvious that he has "been around." It becomes increasingly clear that he has some trust issues. Maybe you are projecting those. (It takes one to know one.)

Early on, he says to his evasive client Brigid O'Shaughnessy (played by Mary Astor), "You won't need much of anybody's help. You're good. Chiefly your eyes I think and that throb you get in your voice when you say things like 'Be generous, Mr. Spade.'"

After the death of his detective-agency partner, we also learn that Sam has been having an affair with the partner's wife. His disgust with her is evident as he instructs his loyal (and obviously lovestruck) secretary to "keep her away" from him. Into Sam's life walks Ms. O'Shaughnessy, who from the outset lies about her name and her reason for seeking detective services. Everything Brigid says throughout the movie is complete bullshit. Yet Sam falls in love. He is protective of Brigid and outsmarts both cops and criminals to protect her from harm.

The last 10 minutes of the movie are the saddest cinema you have ever seen. Sam loves the lying client he now calls "Angel," but he is going to turn her in for her murder of his partner. ("I'm sending you over, Angel.") He ruefully informs her that she may get out in 20 years, and he will be waiting. He expresses hope that they don't decide to hang her pretty neck, in which case he will never forget her. He simply cannot let his partner's murder go unpunished. You admire Sam's principles. But you think he may be a schmuck. This uncertainty is the reason you keep watching.

You are pretty sure that, one way or another, you have always been a schmuck when it come to the opposite sex. You are pretty sure that most of your clients have been as well.

LUNCHTIME IN OAKLAND

O akland can be challenging. You have been here a long time and know where you should and should not go at different times of the day. You are aware of statistics that rank your city neck and neck with Detroit for murder rates and crimes of violence. You are a live-and-let-live kind of guy. But you move among people who do not necessarily share your point of view.

You are a relatively large man. You are not yet old. You flatter yourself that you may even look slightly intimidating to the bad guys in the world. You feel more or less safe in your hood, reasoning that you are a more forbidding target than the women and old folks with whom you transit — that is, if you were a predator, you would choose smaller and older victims than yourself.

It is noon. Four blocks away awaits a perfect hot corned beef on light, crusty rye sandwich. Mustard, mayo. Engorged, wet dill pickle on the side. You have been at work for slightly more than an hour. A man needs midday nourishment, even if he didn't get up until mid-morning. You are walking.

Three dark young men are on the sidewalk, approaching from the opposite direction. One walks 30 feet in front of his companions. He repeatedly glances behind him where the other two young men simply nod. This is not comfortable — at all. Even though it is "broad daylight," there is no one else in the vicinity.

Every drastic course of action (fleeing, yelling, jiving) all seem to have significant downsides. You keep walking as if not worried or afraid. Ignoring the obvious has pretty much been your life's work.

As the first young man passes on your left, he shouts something that sounds like, "Hey ya!" He simultaneously launches his closed fist toward the side of your head, stopping an inch from making contact. The two other "men" whom you now see are probably not even 18 years old. They crack up with laughter as they approach and pass. You are bent over and gasping. Your heart is racing. You mutter obscenities. Everything is intact except your pride. You suspect that you are a practice dummy. Some other poor soul will probably be the recipient of the real attack later today, tonight, or sometime in the near future.

You are not as hungry as you were a few minutes ago. You stay on course. Had you been mugged, there would not have been a big haul. You have all of $18 on you as well as various credit cards that have been pretty much maxed to the limit.

The words of the terminally ill Warren Zevon come to mind: "Enjoy every sandwich." Sounds like a good idea.

Rollo's Deli is a safe haven. Rollo himself is a rotund, happy man in his 60s. Mrs. Rollo has her husband's body type. But she has more facial hair. Phallic cured meats hang from the ceiling. You believe that these dangling meats are decorative since they do not seem to have been replaced in the several years you have come to this establishment. You almost never change your order. Rollo is putting your sandwich together as you cross the threshold.

You slap a 10 spot on the counter, grab your can of Nestea from the refrigerator case, and pick up your bagged corned beef sandwich.

Rollo says, "*Buon appetito*, my friend!" Rollo is probably Armenian. His fake Italian is quaint.

"Get a life!" you zestfully reply.

Everyone smiles as you venture back to the hood.

An old Episcopalian church occupies a large lot to your right. A wrought-iron fence frames the lawn. You open the gate and sit on an iron bench, facing the sidewalk. You dig in to your sandwich, taking small pickle bites as you work. Life is (momentarily) tranquil. You relive the mugging that almost was. You can't decide whether you feel streetwise or emasculated.

Just last week you were witness to some authentic larceny and violence. The CVS near your home is where you pick up your necessities of daily living: paper towels, toothpaste, and rolling papers. You were enjoying a lazy saunter down the aisles, surveying the latest in male-hygiene products, beard/hair dyes, and boxed wine.

A woman screamed, "Stop right there! Get him. *Get him!*"

A child cried out, "Mom — don't!"

You peered cautiously around the aisle. A young woman was chasing a funky-looking bum out the door. As you got to the front window, you watched the woman jump on the bum's back and deliver short, strong blows with her tight little fists to the back of his head. The bum dropped two cartons of cigarettes, presumably stolen. He gathered himself and started swinging a cane he improbably produced from his long coat. He smacked the young woman on her arm and crookedly ran off.

It all happened very quickly. Even though you and a couple of cash-register jockeys made your way out the store to assist, you were not all that fast in doing so. Sure as hell, none of you had any interest in chasing the assailant.

The brave young woman was okay. As you escorted her back into the store, she raised her voice again and cried, "We are a community!" She hugged her confused young son, who had been left standing inside. He looked about six years old and was having some trouble figuring out what had just taken place. Onlookers congratulated the woman's efforts. The police were on their way. Shoppers and store employees chattered excitedly.

You slipped away, thinking that they were all crazy. You imagined that the kid, with a mom like that, would be needing psychotherapy sooner rather than later.

As you sit on the church bench, chewing your corned beef, you reconsider. You have a vague recollection of a catchy phrase about being part of the solution so as to not be part of the problem. But the world and your role in it does not seem that easy to discern nowadays. You distrust solutions. Problems are inevitably more complicated the more you try to deal with them. You think you'll focus on solving the problem of finishing your lunch and keeping pickle juice off your tie.

GETTING TO KNOW LOREN

A new case is usually interesting if not exactly exciting. Most of them do not end up in trial. Most cases settle. That can be a rather bland end. Defendants pay more than they would like. Plaintiffs accept less than they want. No one admits any wrongdoing. Attorneys get paid. Life goes on. But you never know which case is not going to conform to that pattern.

Between opening a file on a new case and the final resolution, there is the work. The aforementioned grunt work is often wasted effort. But you never know ahead of time. It is how most of a litigator's money is made. Sometimes it sticks with you. More often, you forget the whole mess within weeks of its ending.

You are taking the deposition of Loren Patagorkis. You have learned as much as you can from written discovery. You have reviewed employment records, school records, and the little bit of psychological treatment history. Kate is with you, ostensibly to remind you of what you need to ask and to lend a hand with the documents. The real reason she is there is to give her opinion as to how Ms. Patagorkis will come across with jurors — especially females. Kate's bullshit detector is better than yours when it comes to women. As far as you are concerned, most men are greatly impaired in their ability to figure out a woman's credibility. You are certainly one of those men.

You have no intention of asking anything of substance for at least an hour. You are trying to endear yourself to the plaintiff. You have two ways of doing depositions: obvious prick and sneaky one. You are going with sneaky.

You are in the shiny, high-rise office of attorney George Lewis. George looks slick in an expensive suit and a perfect haircut. He smiles constantly and stares with raised eyebrows — kinda scary. If not for the exceptional hair, he would make a good mad scientist in a '30s horror flick. He is generally disinclined to interfere with your questions. Loren is rather plain looking and stylishly attired in a business suit and Manolo shoes. Her blond hair is bluntly cut above the shoulders. She spends some money on her appearance. You smile and shake her hand, holding it a bit too long. She giggles. Good start.

A pretty, young, female court reporter administers the oath and takes down all that is said. Her job is to render verbatim transcriptions of the deposition and interfere only when necessary to get the participants to slow down or not talk over each other.

You go through the deposition preliminaries. Tap dancing.

"Have you ever had your deposition taken before, Loren? May I call you Loren?"

"Sure. This is my first time."

"Everyone has one. As you know, I represent Dr. Thomas. We are here today to find out directly from you, in your own words, what happened with you two. Okay?"

"Yes. Whatever you want to know."

Jesus! Aren't you and Ms. P. a nice couple? Kate is staring into her lap, and Lewis is staring at the ceiling. Everyone is 100 percent aware of what bullshit it all is. Happens every day in exquisite conference rooms just like this. You lay it on thick for an hour or so, going over Loren's childhood, school, and entry into the professional world. You act extremely interested in all of the mundane details of her life before meeting Dr. Thomas.

"Hey, Loren. Thanks for putting up with all these background questions. Do you want to take a break before we get into what this lawsuit is all about?" you ask.

"No. I'm okay."

Here you go. "The complaint states that you and Dr. Thomas had sexual relations. How the heck did you let something like that happen?"

Lewis awakens. "Objection counsel. The form of the question is argumentative and offensive."

"I'm sorry, George. I just want Loren to tell her story any way she wants. Didn't mean to be offensive. Did I offend you, Loren?"

"You can stop calling her Loren now. It's Ms. Patagorkis," erupts Lewis. You make a face of exaggerated surprise. "I'm sorry, Ms. Patagorkis. I guess George is going to make us get all formal now."

Loren laughs. You smile. Lewis seethes. Kate embarrassedly stares into a file. The court reporter shows no emotion as her fingers click away.

"Loren … I mean Ms. Patagorkis … did Dr. Thomas really have sex with you?"

"Yes, he did."

"How many times?"

"Eight."

"Tell me about each one, in as much detail as possible."

She proceeds to do so. Who wore what. Who said what. Who put what where. She is like a medical-school professor describing a surgery technique. This young lady has quite a vivid memory. She recalls the color and weave of the carpet upon which Dr. Thomas scooted her ass. She remembers the brand of condom he used and the unusual sounds he made during orgasm. To her, it was reminiscent of Jackson Browne singing. Foreplay and postcoital cuddles are tediously revisited. Nothing about gray pubic hair though.

You ask, "Do you have any physical evidence of these acts of sex?"

"Like what?"

"Stained clothing? The doctor's undies?"

Demurely, she responds, "No. I can't imagine keeping something like that."

"Did Dr. Thomas have any distinguishing physical features, like scars or moles?"

"I don't think so," she adds, showing the slightest bit of nervousness.

"Is he circumcised?"

"Oh, yes!" she responds as though relieved.

"What color is his pubic hair?"

"Light."

"Light?"

"Well, he's blonde. It's very light."

"Light as in white?"

"I can't say?"

"Why not, Loren?"

Tears form in her eyes. "I don't want to say anything I don't absolutely know to be true. His pubic hair was not dark. He was circumcised. Other than that, I confess that I did not study his penis. I was always caught up in the fantastic experience of loving and being loved. I told him that I loved him. He told me that he loved me too. We talked of spending our lives together. Then, one day, he said it was over. He said that I needed to spread my wings and fly." Her sobbing fills the room.

You glance at the court reporter, who is silently shedding her own tear. This is not going well.

You drag out the questioning for another hour. It is either painful or dull to the point where you can no longer distinguish between the two. You call it a day.

As you walk down Post Street, you glance at Kate. She is grim-faced and not very friendly. You guide her into a restaurant. You order oysters and beer.

"Please tell me she wasn't as credible as I thought," you say.

"That son of a bitch broke her heart," Kate replies.

You apparently need to have it rubbed in. "You bought what she was selling?"

Kate is steely-eyed. "She is absolutely telling the truth."

"Yeah. I thought so," you concede.

"It really doesn't matter," says Kate. "Any woman on a jury would want to hang Dr. Thomas by his gray-haired nuts! By the way, what was all that first-name basis with Loren. You are so embarrassing sometimes."

"As embarrassing as the time I wore the Che Guevara T-shirt to the Bar Association mixer?"

"No. Not that embarrassing."

"Then I should get some credit for improvement. We never came up with any background dirt on her?"

Kate sighs. "No prior claims or lawsuits. No history of psychotherapy. No past diagnosed mental illness. No financial difficulties. Her current psychotherapist says that she has posttraumatic stress disorder due exclusively to therapist sexual abuse."

You take out your cell phone. "Dr Thomas. We just finished Loren's deposition. We need to talk. Can you come in next week?"

BOB

At the end of this shitty day, you retreat to your crumby abode. You are lonely and tired. To make matters worse, there is Bob. As usual, he lies in the middle of your bed. As usual, he eyes you warily and swishes his tail with obvious irritation at your presence. His deep green eyes stare into yours. You are certain that you can discern thousands of years of predatory resentment. Bob's DNA likely contains panther programming that, in its glory years, would have made short work of your measly human form.

You momentarily consider stroking his lush, black fur. But, should you attempt to do so, Bob would leap from the bed and seek solace in the other room or dart out the kitchenette window with its torn screen. It is humiliating to have a pet who avoids you like the plague.

You feed and house this feline. You keep the cat pan more or less clean. You once took him to a vet. The Beatles sang, "Can't Buy Me Love." Maybe Lennon and McCartney owned cats.

Three years ago, you were on a short flight to Los Angles. The beautiful, young woman in the middle seat told you of her devotion to her work at an animal shelter in the Bay Area and expressed her love for and commitment to cats. You replied that you had grown up with cats. (True.) You told her that you preferred cats to dogs and other pets. (Maybe true, although you had sometimes been heard to say that the only good pet was a pet rock.) You earnestly stated that you had recently been considering cat adoption. (Complete fabrication.)

Hoping to connect with your flight friend, and fueled by your second in-flight Bloody Mary, you elaborated on your cat plans and dreams. The woman — Monica — visibly brightened and spoke effusively of cats that would make a "good match" with you. Her eyes glistened. You recognized and respected her sincerity, even though it is a bothersome trait.

"Did you know that shelters are *full* of black cats? People don't take them because of stupid superstitions associating them with witches and bad luck."

You assured Monica that you had no such prejudices. (Never having given it a previous moment of thought.) In fact, you tell her that you had been visualizing owning a black cat like the one with whom you had spent many happy childhood years. (Second total lie.)

Monica asked for your contact information (score!), and you deftly produced your business card.

"Oh! You're a lawyer!" she practically gushed.

This seemed to be proceeding well.

"I'll call you when I get back to San Francisco."

"I really look forward to that," you smoothly replied.

You lost sight of Monica in the grumbling and fumbling of over-head-bin unloading and exit from the plane. Man, she was fast! Truth be told, you were a little inebriated and slow. You did not spot her at baggage claim. Just another entertaining way to pass the time on an airplane. You gave her no more thought. (Okay. Maybe a dream fantasy or two.)

Then, one day, Lawrence announced that you had a visitor – a Ms. Corigliano. "She says that you might not be expecting her. But she has something for you. I think it is alive."

Your heart soared and fell, pretty much simultaneously, as you greeted Monica in the waiting room. You could not help but notice the plastic carton with holes at her feet. Lawrence made no attempt to mask his mirth as you ushered Monica and her gift into your office.

"This cat came into the shelter just a week ago," she explained. "I immediately thought of you. This cat is friendly and very self-contained. He is a 'cool cat.' It seemed to me that he was the kind of cat you wanted. He also reminds me of you. I have a very positive feeling about this match. I am rarely wrong about these things."

You were determined to make the best of this potentially horrible situation. "Are you free for lunch?"

"I would love to. But my fiancé is the jealous type. Let me give you my email address. You can let me know if you have any questions on cat care.

Bob

This fella has been neutered and vaccinated. You need to find a good veterinarian for a follow up. I can give you referrals. Let's for sure keep in touch."

So, you had a cat. You named him Bob.

"That is way more pathetic than it is clever," opined Lawrence.

Kate agreed.

You brought Bob to the office a couple of times. But he preferred his cat carrier to your lap or anything else in the vicinity. You left him at home to contemplate whatever cats think about when all of their worldly needs are met.

You figured out that cats do not respond well to sarcasm.

Typical interaction between you and Bob: "Okay, Bob. I am going to work now. I've got some laundry here. It would be great if you could find the time in your busy day to fold some of this stuff. I'll show you how. Match the seams on the pants, pull up the crotch, and fold a couple of times. Got it? The shirts need to be on hangars — probably outside of your range. I don't mean to mock your lack of height. But maybe you could just fold them any way you can manage. As to the socks and underwear, simply separate them from the rest, and I will put them in the drawers later. We good?"

Bob stares into your eyes. You would like to believe that he would help you in some way if he could. To pull his weight a bit. No. He wants you to drop dead. He gathers himself, jumps from the bed, and struts from the room with his tail at high sail. No confrontation. Just contempt.

As you take over Bob's daytime sanctuary, you remember the instruction that your mother tried to instill and that your interactions with Monica Corigliano have reinforced: "Don't talk to strangers!"

On the other hand, it occurs to you that Monica was right. Bob and you are a good match.

GETTING TO KNOW LOIS

By every indication, Dr. Golden's long-time patient Lois Sutcliffe has had a miserable life from her teen years forward. You know that lots of people must have equally miserable or worse existences. But most people do not have them so well documented. Lois has been going to psychiatrists and psychologists since she was in high school. You have accumulated hundreds of pages of records from them.

At age 16, Lois was sent to a psychiatrist to help with her fits of depression and intermittent rage. She had been obsessed with a boy who had asked her on a date and then shunned her subsequent attempts at contact. Lois entered into a depressive state, culminating in a suicide attempt — superficial cutting of her wrists. From that time on, Lois has been on some form of psychotropic medication.

She finished high school with reasonably good grades and was admitted to a woman's college of some repute. Her studies were twice interrupted by psychiatric hospitalizations that followed suicide attempts. She bounced from therapist to therapist, typically ending treatment on bad terms with her providers. She accused them of negligence and incompetence. These attacks were variously documented or implied in the many records you review. By graduation, Lois had been in therapy with no less than a dozen different mental health professionals.

Lois took the LSAT and applied to law schools unsuccessfully. Her exam score and grades were high enough to gain entry to mid-level law schools. But she had set her sights unrealistically high. Her failure to be admitted to an Ivy League law school was, she believed, due to discrimination about her mental difficulties. She wrote letters to law-school administrators, threatening litigation.

She moved to California — initially Los Angeles. She stayed just long enough for one emergency-room visit. She was committed involuntarily as a danger to herself and discharged after 72 hours.

Finally, Lois landed in San Jose and found Dr. Golden. His records are not detailed. But they do reflect long-standing and repetitive problems for Lois in finding any kind of stable personal or professional relationship. Her distrust of others and incredibly demanding behavior were not attractive presentations. She was unhappy, frequently suicidal, and angry. In Dr. Golden, she seems to have found someone who would tolerate her demands and support her through tough times. She stayed out of mental hospitals, did not try to kill herself, and held down low-paying but stable clerical jobs. Dr. Golden worked with her for 15 years. He did not cure her. But he seems to have helped her find a way to get by.

You take Lois's deposition. She is an intense woman with dark hair and eyes. She is scrawny and a bit unkempt. You would describe her as having "below-average jury appeal." She looks like she could explode at any moment. You have taken the depositions of quite a few angry women. Still, Lois scares you a bit. Schiff is characteristically bombastic and obstructive. You think he has probably been that way since he was born. He acts out whether there is any reason to do so. You could easily finish the deposition in a day. But all of the objections, speeches, and breaks taken by opposing counsel require a second day to complete the telling of Lois's tale. Lois tells it, alternately sobbing and raging.

The upshot is that she began seeing Dr. Golden for medication and psychotherapy after having had a brief encounter with him during one of a series of psychiatric hospitalizations. Lois had been frequently suicidal, leading to emergency-room visits and involuntary commitment in psychiatric wards. Dr. Golden was on staff at one of these hospitals and made rounds for Lois's attending psychiatrist one day. He was considerate and friendly. He treated her like a "real person" and not a crazy one. Lois took note of his name and gave him a call after her discharge. Lois's current psychiatrist was more than pleased to transfer her care. Lois was thrilled that Dr. Golden had an opening in his private practice. In her view, he had consistently accommodated her special needs throughout the years of working together.

This began 15 years of abuse, so said Lois. "Oh, he was sneaky. He made me trust him and then lowered the boom! He made me completely dependent on him for everything. But ultimately it was I who had to meet his needs on a moment's notice. It wasn't sexual at first. But, over time, we became close physically as well as spiritually. At least that is what he led me to believe!"

According to Lois, treatment with Dr. Golden was initially appropriate and beneficial. He adjusted her medications, reducing the doses of some and taking her completely off others. He encouraged her to pursue employment opportunities and to take time off from her repeated attempts to take the bar exam. He supported her application to work at the nearby university library and wrote a letter of recommendation on her behalf. She got the job. And, with Dr. Golden's help, including some between-session phone contacts, kept it. She lived independently, managed her daily affairs, negotiated problems at work, and refrained from suicidal actions. She was by no means "happy." But she admits to being stable.

She attributes her early success to Dr. Golden's willingness to give her help whenever she needed it. "He would always talk me through a crisis — day or night."

Gradually, according to Lois, Dr. Golden changed. He talked of his own life and problems. He was unhappy in his marriage. He questioned his choice of profession. He sought out Lois after business hours. She became his "shoulder to cry on." He began to hug, stroke, and kiss her during sessions, leading to sexual intercourse on multiple occasions — in the office and at Lois's apartment. (There were no known witnesses to any of these social or sexual encounters.) Whenever you press for details of this sexual activity, Lois becomes agitated and Schiff goes into his act. Frankly, he wears you down. Lois is so pathetic that you see no reason to prolong things. You know she is full of shit. You can feel it in your bones.

As to Dr. Golden's alleged personal disclosures, Lois is an encyclopedia. She can recite Dr. Golden's history from childhood forward: schools attended, family members, professional accomplishments, publications, hobbies (he liked skeet shooting and was a member of a shooting club), and his unhappy and unsatisfying first marriage followed by an ill-advised second union with "that simpleton Laura." Most of all, Lois recalls his fervent love for one Lois Sutcliffe. (None of this makes the slightest bit of sense to you. From a male's perspective, Laura gets the guy's heart 101 out of 100 times over plain, crazy Lois.)

How was she harmed by all of this? "He needed to keep me in my place. He talked me out of becoming a lawyer. He had me at his beck and call. He ruined any chance I had at a decent life. He used me for sex whenever he wanted. I was his slave." On top of that, Lois has calculated the insurance money and copays received by Dr. Golden over the course of treatment: more than $200,000.

Lois acknowledges that she did stay out of hospitals for the time she was with Dr. Golden and that she has maintained employment. Those years were, however, marred by misery and despair beyond anything she had previously experienced. (Yeah, right.)

The news of Dr. Golden's death hit Lois hard. She had no knowledge of him having been ill. She admitted that she had tried to contact Dr. Golden's family after his death to express sympathy and to find out details of the funeral. She had been rebuffed and could not understand why.

Her life spiraled downward. She could not keep up with her job duties and was terminated. She became suicidal and was repeatedly hospitalized. During one commitment, she spoke at length to a psychiatrist she had never before met. She talked obsessively about the loss of Dr. Golden. This new doctor posed the question as to whether her relationship had been "something more" than patient and doctor. Finally, someone understood! Yes. There was more … *much* more. She told the doctor everything, which was duly noted in her hospital chart. She and Dr. Golden were friends and lovers. Now she had nothing to show for her years of devotion and silence. Soon after, Lois sought out an attorney.

After Lois and her attorney depart, you feel sullied. Everything you have heard over the course of two days feels like it came from a sick, altered universe. Your cerebral cortex analyzes and rejects everything about Lois and her Dr. Golden fantasy. You think it likely that a jury will someday see things the same way.

You report Lois's testimony to the insurer and to Laura Golden. You know that Laura will be upset, so you go out of your way to express your confidence that Lois will ultimately fail in her mercenary quest. Laura is "most appreciative" of your efforts. You wonder how appreciative that might be.

Driving home, you listen to an oldies radio station with The Kinks doing, "Till the End of the Day":

Baby, I feel good
From the moment I arise
Feel good from morning
Till the end of the day
Till the end of the day

Yeah, you and me
We live this life
From when we get up
Till we go to sleep at night
You and me were free
We do as we please, yeah
From morning, till the end of the day
Till the end of the day

You think of the last time that this kind of naiveté made the slightest sense to you. The song is barely over two minutes long. The guitar solo is about 12 seconds. You cannot think of simpler, less challenging words and music. You love it.

You follow up with other people whose paths Lois has crossed. None of these people are happy about their experiences in that regard.

Over the years with Dr. Golden, Lois had also seen several other local psychiatrists. These were all solo practitioners, like Dr. Golden, who accepted emergency calls for each other and provided patient coverage during each other's vacations and illnesses. Whenever Dr. Golden went out of town, Lois became particularly needy. All of the MDs in the coverage group knew Lois. They had all, in one way or another, tried to ease her through Dr. Golden's absences. You vow to visit them all. After obtaining Lois's written authorizations, you do so.

You make appointments with and meet Drs. Severson, Miller, Witgang, Potter, and Gonzaga. They uniformly extoll the virtues and high ethics of Dr. Golden. If they fault him at all, it is only for the fact that he cared too much and hung in with difficult patients who were demanding but not significantly improving. Lois was the obvious case in point.

In one way or another, they all communicate their disdain for Lois.

"In my hospital training years, she is the kind of patient we referred to as a GOMER," says Dr. Potter, a sprightly, 80-year-old elf.

You raise an eyebrow in what you imagine to be a look of collegial curiosity, even though you know the tired acronym. "Meaning?"

"Get Out of My Emergency Room," he cackles. "People like Lois take up inordinate amounts of time, are abusive and demanding, and never get better. They suck the life out of you. They are mentally ill. But not the kind of ill anyone in the profession wants to spend time with."

"Maybe a psychiatrist would if he were getting some other kind of payback," you venture.

Dr. Potter glares at you indignantly. "You don't know your client if you think that was even a possibility for Lucas. That man was 100 percent dedicated to his patients, and I have no problem getting on a witness stand to say so."

"Cool. I was just being a devil's advocate. Thanks for being willing to stand up for your colleague."

Dr. Cheryl Severson is the only female in the bunch of Dr. Golden's cronies. She is a sharp-featured septuagenarian whose office is chrome sleek and modern. Dr. Severson's contacts with Lois Sutcliffe were memorably contentious and unpleasant. Dr. Golden had asked that Dr. Severson consider accepting a transfer of Lois's care. He expressed the thought that the therapist-transference issues, which were so obviously at play with Lois, might be diminished and controlled if her doctor were a woman. Theoretically, this made sense to Dr. Severson. Lois expressed her understanding as well. But the two of them were "oil and water" from the outset.

"Everything I said was challenged by Lois. She was, by far, the most negative and unreceptive person with whom I have ever interacted. She had no desire whatsoever to work with me."

"Did she ever talk about Dr. Golden?"

"Is the Pope Catholic?"

"I think that is one of the job requirements … at least on paper."

Severson continues. "Lois compared everything I said to what Dr. Golden would have said instead. I got second place across the board. I tried to keep the therapy going, out of respect for Lucas. But it was doomed from the start. Lois was just too obsessed with her white knight — Lucas Golden."

"Didn't that ever strike you as a little weird?"

Dr. Severson replies without hesitation. "No. I think it was textbook borderline obsession with a fantasized savior. And yes, I will testify to that opinion."

Drs. Miller and Potter are similarly effusive about Dr. Golden. They are also more or less eager to testify at trial and trash Lois Sutcliffe. These are your kind of people, and you shamelessly pander to them.

Dr. Witgang is a tweed-attired, pipe-smoking 70-year-old with amazingly long, gray hair that is growing straight out of his ears, seemingly defying the laws of gravity. As disconcerting as that look is, it more or less matches his burly gray eyebrows. You are pretty sure that this is a fellow who long ago stopped caring about what he saw when he looked in the mirror. Or he has a significant vision defect. Everything about his initial impression shouts, "Curmudgeon." He turns out, however, to be cordial and soft spoken. He speaks of Dr. Golden with obvious respect and affection. He describes Lois as a "very challenging" young woman whose claims in the lawsuit are "absurd."

"Tragically, her love for her psychiatrist transformed into a fantasy world in which she was both sought after by the doctor and then cruelly exploited and abandoned. Freud and Jung both described this phenomenon in detail. It has been repeated in thousands of patient/therapist dyads ever since."

Witgang relights his stupidly large pipe and continues. "I knew Lucas Golden as a psychiatrist and a friend. Ms. Sutcliffe's allegations are impossible. Lucas cared for the welfare of his patients. But he absolutely loved his wife. He had Laura's name on his lips as he died. He was a devoted father to all his children. He was probably the most ethical and responsible person I have ever known."

You eat this stuff up. "Dr. Witgang, this is *exactly* what I need to convey to a jury. I think you would be a great witness as to Dr. Golden's integrity and the psychodynamics that explain Lois's false claim against him."

Dr. Witgang peers at you searchingly. "I don't think you want me to be a witness at trial."

"Sure, I do. Why not?"

"Well, you know of course that Laura was a former patient of Lucas. I referred her to him. For a long time, I have been a family friend. I would hate to be put in a position where the opposition attorney asks questions about Lucas and Laura. People could easily misunderstand."

You suppress a gulp. "You mean people might misunderstand that Dr. Golden had at least once before crossed the line with a patient and became her lover?"

Witgang's gigantic eyebrows droop, and he looks mopey. "It wasn't like that. But who would believe it? Lucas and Laura ended their professional relationship well before they began their personal one. And Laura does not have a personality disorder or a chronic disability. There was absolutely no question of exploitation."

You are stunned but want to be conciliatory. "Well, you're probably right. Jurors won't appreciate the differences."

Witgang is now more energetic and earnest. "I do have my records regarding Lois. They are very comprehensive, if I do say so myself. They clearly document Lois's borderline personality and pathological attachment to Dr. Golden. Can't you make some use of them without me having to testify in person?"

You consider. "I'm not sure. I guess I can give them to my experts and have them communicate them to the jury. But I need to tell you something. I did not know that Laura had been Dr. Golden's patient. I'm feeling a little uneasy right now."

Dr. Witgang proceeds to talk you down. He is good. His voice is like sonic Valium. He explains that the ethics of therapist relationships with former patients have changed over the years. (You, more than just about anyone, already know that.) Dr. Witgang points out that, in years past, many famous psychiatrists married their patients without anyone claiming that something was amiss. He assures me that everything Lucas did vis-à-vis Laura was in her best interest and with the consultation of another professional (i.e., him).

"Please don't tell Laura about the gaffe I have made. I had no right to disclose her medical information. I just thought you knew. No one else needs to. Don't you agree?"

You guess you do.

PROTECTING LAURA

S chiff has subpoenaed Laura Golden for a deposition. You spend a tense couple of hours with her in her home. She is jittery as you explain the deposition process. Repeatedly, she seems on the verge of tears. You are trying to reassure her that you will be at her side, making sure that Schiff does not abuse her in any way. But you are also trying to let her know just how intrusive and obnoxious he will be. The au pair is playing with David in the backyard. Laura repeatedly glances in their direction as though they might be making an escape without her vigilance. She is an anxious mom.

You do not divulge that you know she was once her husband's patient. Instead, you tell her that there is nothing about her relationship with Lucas that is relevant to the lawsuit and that you will object to any attempts by Schiff to ask questions about that topic. On the other hand, what Laura knows about Lucas's taking calls from the patient who almost certainly was Lois is relevant. It is also relevant — and useful — for Laura to testify regarding Lucas's dedication to his patients and the professionalism he showed in not telling anyone, including her, about their cases. That could prove invaluable at trial since Lucas will obviously not be able to speak on his own behalf.

You volunteer to drive Laura to and from the deposition. You do not always offer chauffer service. You do when you think your client needs extra support. Do you have ulterior motives? Are there any other kind?

You attempt to assuage her fear and anxiety. Conversation turns to David and his growth and interests. Laura mentions Adam and the other golden son but only in passing. She comments briefly on the first Mrs. Golden — Nancy — and their civil relationship. Laura tells you that she had a great deal of initial reluctance to date a man so much older than herself but that Lucas had won her over with his sincerity and his obvious sense of responsibility to the family he had left behind. You do not pry. You assure Laura that you will protect her from having to answer any questions regarding her family.

The deposition takes place in Schiff's office. It strikes you that you are about to imitate Schiff. You will be consciously interfering with and undermining the deposition. You are going to pick fights. This will be fun in a sick sort of way. You let Schiff know that the deposition will be limited to two hours and that he will need to seek a court order if he wants to continue at a later date. You spend five minutes making objections on the record to the deposition and state your intent to terminate exactly at the end of the two hours, which you are arbitrarily allotting. Schiff spends five minutes more arguing about what you have said. Good. Ten minutes down, 110 to go.

Schiff asks Laura basic background questions. You object to almost every one of them. You also take breaks to confer with Laura off the record. Schiff is beside himself. You object to his tone of voice and volume. You make a formal record of his threatening postures and facial expressions. You state your intent to terminate the deposition early if his behavior does not immediately become more professional. The two of you trade insults and arguments. Another 40 minutes have passed.

Through all of this, Laura remains quiet. But she is also quite obviously shaken. You know in your heart of hearts that Schiff is sensing that Laura is psychologically frail. He is aware that your behavior is uncharacteristic. He is anything but stupid.

Schiff sits back and appears to contemplate. "How did you and Dr. Golden first meet?"

You hold up your hand to Laura and quickly interject. "Objection. The question is not reasonably calculated to lead to the discovery of admissible evidence. It invades my client's privacy. It is harassment."

Schiff looks at you and exposes a big, shit-eating grin. He knows! You know he knows, and he knows you know. Schiff stands up and thanks Laura for her time. You depart with a bad, bad feeling in your gut. You drive Laura home, chatting benignly about child rearing and recent movies. You pretend that everything has gone well as you walk Laura to her door and say goodbye. You are pretty sure that she is not as oblivious as she seems.

The next week, you meet Adam Golden alone. You want to find out what he knows about Laura and his father. Not much according to him. He describes Dr. Golden as a private and circumspect man. He tells you of a lecture he once received from his father about patient confidentiality. He does not know anything about how Laura and Dr. Golden met except that it was through some mutual acquaintances. He believes that his father and Laura were very much in love. He praises his father as a provider to his family and a supporter of his desire to become a physician. You still like this young guy and think he might be one of those golden nuggets as a trial witness. You realize that you want to take advantage of his ignorance regarding Laura having been a patient of his father. You have no obligation to clue him in and cannot imagine how that would help your cause. It is not as if you have unquestioning respect for the medical profession, let alone psychiatry. But you believe in Dr. Golden's innocence. His friends, his son, and his wife couldn't all hold him in such regard if he were a putz. (Like many shrinks you know.)

Oddly, you encounter one of the putz-like examples the very next day. You lunch regularly at Dr. Yum's — a Chinese restaurant that you believe epitomizes the perfect balance of good versus questionable taste in every sense of the word. You are not a foodie. But you sure think a lot about food. California is full of mediocre Chinese cuisine, indifferently prepared with cheap ingredients. Of course, there are also exquisitely crafted Chinese meals with the best and freshest components. You look for and patronize the places that fall in between. You like expertly made humble dishes. Not fancy but not overly funky. You think it is a yin-yang kind of thing. You have a vague understanding of many philosophies with no solid under-standing of any. Being a lawyer has been a great way to perpetuate being a dilettante. You dislike people who do the kind of intellectual posturing to which you are prone. You don't actually know your yin from your yang. But no one in California would ever question your use of those terms.

Anyway, Dr. Yum's serves a dynamite curry chicken, even though the chicken is a little on the scrappy side. You surmise that it is so good because it is "on the border" of good taste. If it were a little less fatty, there would be a little less flavor. A little more gristle would be a turnoff. Borderline dining. You are convinced that you are onto something here. But no one with whom you have shared your theory seems convinced or interested.

Dr. Yum's is located on a dirty Oakland side street. But the dining area is clean. Patrons with functioning olfactory senses would not stay in the restroom any longer than necessary. But the toilet (usually) works. The waiters are efficient and polite. A couple of the women are "borderline" babes. And, of course, the price is right: $5.99 for the lunch special, including soup, egg roll, orange wedges, and the cookie with your fortune inside. You feel quite comfortable here.

But today is a drag because there is a man in the booth behind you, loudly holding a conversation with the aid of his Bluetooth mechanism. He is eating at the same time, so the slurping and chomping mix unpleasantly with his booming voice. You are not attempting to eavesdrop. You would pay good money for earplugs. The one-sided conversation penetrates your defenses and your two glasses of Riesling. (You always order the cheapest wine in these establishments. The most expensive is never appreciably better.)

"What da hell do you want me ta do about it anyway?" the loudmouth slurps and yells. "I've already got her loaded up on enough Seroquel to drop a fuckin' rhino!"

You can't resist looking over your shoulder.

The balding, red-faced man pauses for a moment, shoves a forkful of pot stickers in his mouth, and continues. "Yeah, yeah, yeah. *You* try to get her into inpatient care. She agrees one moment, and then fights ya the next. What a pain in the ass! The husband's a wimp! The parents pay the bills, praise God. But they're not much help either." He stops to chew and then continues. "Sure. Let's max out the Remeron. I'll sign off on whadever the fuck you need."

You understand, as the other nearby diners may not, that this guy is a psychiatrist discussing medications for psychosis and depression. You have spent a lot of time with these fellows. The only thing surprising to you is that he is so freely expressing himself in public. He probably thinks that he is the only person in the joint who went to college. You give him your special Dr. Yum's stank eye with no apparent effect. You fantasize corrective interactions you might have with Dr. Bluetooth. You leave quickly with only a wink at one of the waitresses. There are bigger fish to fry.

THINKING OF LAURA

L aura Golden is on your mind. She has sent a thank-you note. On the front of the card is a garden of flowers in the middle of which is a small, wooden bench. The bench is pristine. You know nothing about trees or lumber. But you bet that this is an expensive bench crafted from the finest wood. Oak? Old-forest redwood? Why are you thinking about wood? Who cares about wood? You imagine Laura on that bench. Maybe she is wearing a gauzy sundress. Maybe she is holding a drink with a parasol in it. Maybe you are wedged in beside her.

You don't know anything about flowers either. But you are pretty sure that these are upscale, Atherton flowers — not the kind of plants you could purchase at a Target garden store. The preprinted "Thank You for Being Such a Good Friend" message is followed by Laura's handwritten note: "I am comforted by your counsel, counselor."

If you were a teenage girl, you might feel faint. You may, in fact, be feeling faint anyway. But you are also thinking lewd thoughts.

If you were a psychiatrist, these kinds of thoughts about a client could prompt realization of the need to consider termination of the relationship. At least, this is what the modern boundary police contend. Most current-day psychotherapists would recommend that a doctor with sexual fantasies about his or her client seek consultation with another doctor. You think you know what most often happens. Psychotherapists delude themselves with the same kind of mental gymnastics and denial that other mortals employ. They find ways to rationalize the continuation of interactions that make them feel good. Most humans enjoy being in the company of other humans who are sexually exciting. Lizard brain trumps frontal lobe. Pretend all you want. You and your clientele know better.

In Freud's day, psychoanalysts frequently became personally and sexually involved with their patients. Freud characterized the sex as a "mistake" — not an ethical capital offense. He cautioned his peers to not take it personally when a client fell in love with her doctor. And not to do likewise because it usually distorted the focus of the treatment. Over the years, thousands of (usually male) psychotherapists bedded their (mostly female) patients. As Dr. Witgang had noted, some married each other. Many remained clients or close friends for years.

In the 1980s, something dramatic happened. Researchers systematically revealed, primarily by questionnaires given to therapists, that sexual contact with patients was incredibly common. (Hats off to Dr. Kenneth Pope!) More than 12 percent of psychotherapists admitted having had sex at least one time with a patient. Some researchers came up with substantially larger estimates. In and of itself, these might just have been interesting findings. But they aroused a feminist-fueled rage at the "exploitation" inherently involved.

One of the great consumer-driven movements of all time resulted in legislation and ethics-code revisions to address the situation. Psychotherapist/patient sexual contact was condemned, sanctioned, and criminalized. A rather commonplace and seemingly accepted act was transformed into a heinous, career-ending, and criminal one. Good for your business, you must admit.

You have always rebelled against black-and-white thinking. You are more of a shades-of-gray kinda guy. Still, the new-order rules make sense to you. For doctors. It has nothing to do with you, does it?

HOME LIFE

You direct your attention to Dr. Thomas. You trust Kate's instincts. You agree that Loren Patagorkis will make a convincing witness. You think that Dr. Thomas is probably full of shit. But you have a job to do on his behalf, and you are going to do it — even if your approach is a little unorthodox. You sometimes congratulate yourself on being so out of the box. You appreciate your own wild imagination. You wonder whether you should have watched so many Buñuel films in your younger days. You wonder whether drugs and alcohol have dampened the ability of your amygdala to properly process your emotions. You wonder that all the time.

You return home to your rundown bungalow in the downwardly mobile part of the city. This may once have been a cozy Oakland neighborhood. But now they are low-rent units wedged between a 7-Eleven and a freeway on ramp.

Aaron, the occupant of the adjacent cottage, runs up excitedly. He is a child-like 35-year-old in T-shirt and jeans. "Hey, Dude. You know that new cute one — Marcia?"

"The tenant in 4-A?"

"Yeah. The one with the Dodge Charger. I got a call from Walgreen's pharmacy. Marcia picked up my medication. They said she was getting it for me. They were checking to make sure. I think she must have found one of my prescription bottles in the dumpster."

You envisage the tenant in question. She looks like an anorexic teenager with inexplicably large breasts. She seems perpetually buzzed. Goodlooking young women get away with this type of thing, in your humble opinion.

"I'm sorry to hear that," you offer. "What kind of medication was it, Aaron?"

Aaron twitches. "My Xanax."

"Well, I'm sure the pharmacy will refill it."

Aaron looks panicked. "I'd have to rat on Marcia. I don't want to get anyone in trouble. I think I'll have to gut this month out."

You sympathize. "You're a good guy, Aaron. But have you ever heard of 'enabling' an addict? You might be doing us all a favor by reporting it. People who steal drugs usually steal other stuff too."

"You are bumming me out, Dude. I'm not about to cause a scene. I thought you might have a few tranqs lying around that you could spot me."

"Sorry, Aaron. Wrong decade. Hang in there." You retreat. There probably are a few expired benzodiazepines somewhere in an old backpack. You do not want to be part of the housing complex supply chain.

You enter your small dwelling, sit in front of the TV, and turn on a basketball game without the sound. You are considering the music you want to accompany the athletic display, debating between the lightning pace of Al Di Meola's guitar or the comforting bark of Johnny Cash. The phone rings before you have made your choice. It is your 10-year-old daughter Miranda.

"Hi there, Miro. How was your day?"

She asks about yours.

"Me? I've been working on a couple of hot new cases."

"More psychotherapists having sex with their patients?" she teases.

She is cute but too fucking precocious at times. "Allegedly."

"Dad, dual relationships impair the professional's objectivity!"

"You've been talking to your mother again. Have you finished your homework?"

"Yep. I'll see you this weekend. What are you doing the rest of the evening?"

"I'm going to have a drink, maybe two. Bye darling."

"Bye, Daddy. I'm here if you need me."

"I'm the one who is supposed to say that!"

You consider the wisdom of children with old souls versus the hard-won knowledge of the middle-aged man with an immature spiritual life. You choose the Man in Black for your evening companion.

LIE DETECTING

D r. Thomas has arrived for your meeting. He is waiting in the conference room. You are late again. When you arrive at the Victorian, Kate and Lawrence are in the middle of a vigorous game of Slapjack at Lawrence's desk. It is difficult to express your disapproval of their childishness given your tardiness. You are like a schoolteacher, ruefully accepting that you have lost control of the classroom.

You choose to ignore the delinquents and proceed to the encounter with Dr. Thomas. This is what is sometimes referred to as a "come-to-Jesus meeting."

You lay it on the line with your client. "Doctor, I don't like beating around the bush. It doesn't look good. Loren makes a very favorable witness impression. She describes her sexual encounters with you in excruciating detail. She's believable. She doesn't seem crazy. She has no history of other claims or lawsuits. She was obviously in love with you. Your late sessions, followed by computer sharing, and your flat-tire rescue episode are just the kind of thing that Lewis's expert witnesses will use to prove your poor boundaries with patients. Loren correctly identifies you as circumcised. She is vague as to pubic-hair color but not enough to impact her credibility. Your recordkeeping is below standard, which proves nothing in and of itself. But it is consistent with a therapist who is less than totally professional. It is still a she said/he said case. But a jury will more than likely believe what *she* says. By the way, are you a Jackson Browne fan?"

"Huh?"

"Never mind."

You definitely have the doctor's attention. His eyes are open wide as he asks, "What do we do? How do I deal with this mess?"

More coming to the Lord. "You can roll the dice and go to trial. Or you can settle the case. You have no insurance. What assets do you have?"

"I have a house with very little equity. I have about $20,000 in savings and my pride and joy — a 27-foot sailboat. I keep it docked in Sausalito. That's where I spend my weekends and vacations. I own it free and clear."

You find it hard to fathom that your client may not yet have considered the financial consequences. "Going to trial will take all of your cash, at the very least. Losing at trial means that Ms. Patagorkis can force the sale of your assets, including your boat. It might make the most sense to sell the yacht yourself. Get the best price possible in order to fund a settlement."

Dr. Thomas is hyperventilating. "This can't be happening! I am innocent! Remember, I said that I would take a lie-detector test."

A corollary to the come-to-Jesus speech is the call-the-bluff gambit. "Let's do it then. I'll set up a lie detector."

"I thought you said that it was not admissible in court," Doctor T. backtracks.

"It's not. But let's just see how you do. We might be able to make some use of it. I will call a friend of mine in the D.A.'s office and get a referral."

Now the doctor's eyes have narrowed. "You think I had sex with her. Don't you?"

You ease up. "That is not how my brain works. I do however think that *other* people will believe that you had your way with her. My job is to come up with reasons for them not to have that belief. Let's do the polygraph and see what happens."

BROKEN DREAMS

A new case is always just a phone call away. You sometimes take calls that are promising but turn out to be duds. Sometimes even the duds stick with you.

"Hi. My name is Dr. Jim Paris. I am a psychologist down here in Los Angeles. My friend Dr. Burstein told me about you. Said you were the person to help me with this little problem I'm having. I'm very good at what I do. My colleagues speak very highly of me. I've never experienced anything like this before."

The bells are ringing in your head. Nobody calls you with "little" problems from L.A. You are fundamentally suspicious of people who tell you how "good" they are, especially within the first 60 seconds of their call.

"What kind of problem are we talking about, Dr. Paris?"

"The thing is that I'm actually being sued by a former patient! She's totally crazy. This is a shakedown for money. That's what it is."

"Yes. Sometimes they are."

"They are *what*?"

"Crazy. Or shaking you down for money. Or both."

"I can't begin to tell you all the things I did for this woman. I've gone way above and beyond the normal bounds to help her get some kind of life … to get on track. Now it's all just about money. I can't believe it."

You can. "Sounds complicated. Let me get some basic information. You mentioned being sued. Have you been served with a civil complaint — a lawsuit?"

"Yes. Three weeks ago."

"Okay. A response needs to be filed with the court in a pretty short period of time, usually 30 days from when you first received the written complaint. What was the date when you were served?"

"Exactly three weeks ago. Or four. Maybe a little more."

"Can you fax or scan me the complaint right away?"

"I can do that."

"Why don't you start at the begining. Tell me about your practice. Tell me about this patient — when you started treating her and when it ended. What were her problems, her diagnosis, and the general course of treatment? Of course, tell me anything unusual that may have led to the complaint."

"Unusual? *Hah!* I can't begin to tell you how she fucked me over!"

"Let's start with the reason she was in treatment."

"Crazy bitch! She had some longstanding affiliation issues, unhappiness in her job, and no ability to maintain a relationship with a man. She was depressed — really a fuckin' mess. Classic borderline personality. I gave her a structure. Our work was paying off splendidly. Her whole existence turned around. I'm really proud of what I can accomplish. I'm very, *very* good at what I do. Did I tell you that?"

"Uh huh."

"Her name is Sharon. Miserable, miserable person. Pretty good looking but just makes things tough for herself. Very down on everything and everybody. Lot of distrust … you know the type. She's so goddamn borderline! But I guess I asked for it. She's been so empowered by my treatment that now she's got the cajones to come after me for money! Christ, it's just so hard to believe after all I've done for her."

"How long was Sharon your patient?"

"Three years, more or less."

"Ending how long ago?"

"Well, that's hard to say. I stopped charging for my services about a year ago. We have had more of a barter arrangement. But we continued the therapeutic work."

"Oh?"

"It's a long story."

"I've got time. I would like to get an understanding of what this is all about."

"Okay. Thirty-five-year-old female. Crappy job with some nonprofit bozos. No boyfriend. Bad family support. History of conventional psychotherapy — no help at all. She was depressed, had some doofus family practitioner loading her up with a bunch of Prozac and Valium. She had no sense of purpose. She was going through life, week to week, with no vision. You know what I mean?"

Yes. You sure do.

"No spiritual values. I don't just do psychotherapy, by the way, even though I get very good results doing my own eclectic mix of cognitive, behavioral, and psychodynamic models. I find it often useful to incorporate my skills as a Buddhist monk in training. It makes for a very potent intervention. Very powerful stuff. I am very accomplished with just this kind of patient."

Your ringing bells have now given way to nausea. Mixing psychotherapy and religion are indigestible for you.

"Anyway, Sharon responded well to the treatment, and I upped it to two times a week. I started giving her some meaningful tasks. She had asked if there were things she could do to help me out in the office. I have a home office, by the way. We came up with mutually beneficial tasks for her and somewhat for me. Are you familiar with Morita psychotherapy? It's Japanese Zen oriented. You focus on your mundane chore and do it very, very well. Gradually, you encounter and appreciate the greater meanings of the universe and your place in it."

"What sort of tasks?"

"Just clerical things at first. Some organizing of the office. Filing. Filling out some insurance forms for patients. Tidying up. Like I said, my office is in my home, so there were some other tasks. I guess you'd call them 'household' tasks. She helped some with the kids now and then. Did I mention that I'm divorced? I have custody two days a week. My kids are terrific. Sharon took to them right away, and they really liked her too."

"Your patient was babysitting for you?"

"You could describe it that way. It was really an extension of the therapy and the connection we had established."

"And she worked on your other patients' files?"

After a long pause, Dr. Paris says, "Yes."

There is something so clueless about this guy that you are actually feeling as though you should reach through the phone and slap him. But you have a gentle side. "Doctor, I don't want you to take this the wrong way. Some people might say that the boundaries of your therapy were crossed. Do you keep up with your continuing education requirements?"

"Funny you should ask that. I have done several of those online ethics courses to get the necessary credits for renewal of my license. Sharon took the last one for me."

"She completed the online ethics course in your name?"

"Yeah. Kind of ironic, now that I think about it."

You are rarely speechless with potential clients. For a moment, you *are* speechless. You continue. "Tell me about the lawsuit."

"The complaint says that I 'abused the transference phenomenom and negligently and intentionally harmed plaintiff by various and repeated acts of sexual contact with defendant and his friends.' There's a lot of other stuff. But that's probably the most provocative sounding."

"Is it accurate that you had sex with Sharon?"

"Yes, but it always had a therapeutic goal."

"What was that about your friends?"

"That only happened twice, maybe three times. She was totally up for it. Totally consensual and consistent within the context of our work."

"Come again?" You immediately regret your choice of words.

"Sexual feelings are not something that psychotherapists should shy away from nor do they help patients who have relationship issues by adopting rigid taboos within the therapeutic envelope."

"Doctor, in the view of most mental-health professionals, and certainly the view of the Board of Psychology, a patient cannot give meaningful consent to engage in sex with a psychotherapist. And psychotherapy can never include sexual contact. I'm not trying to be critical of you, but surely you are aware of that prevalent view." At least here on planet Earth.

"It's not as if this happens with all my patients. This was an unusual set of conditions. And the results were very, very good. Sharon came out of her negative space. I've paid a steep price already. And now this goddamn law-suit! I should be suing her!"

"I don't think I am following you."

"She broke my dick! I swear to *God*, she broke it!"

"Doctor … if you are a doctor … I am starting to have my doubts as to whether this phone call is on the up and up. Who did you say referred you to me?"

"Dr. Burstein over in Marina del Rey. Look, I know this sounds incred-ible, but it's absolutely true. You can look it up. A penile fracture is what they call it. It's not as uncommon as you might think. It's a blunt-force injury. Hurts like a son of a bitch, and now I've got a permanent bend to the right. The medical literature associates it with overly aggressive female action while in the dominant position. It may have been some form of unconscious acting out on Sharon's part. I don't know. But I do know that, when it happened and as far I was concerned, treatment was over. If I can't sue her for it, I should at least be entitled to use it in my defense."

"Actually, Doctor, I think not."

"Well, thanks for your time then. I'll be talking to a couple of other attorneys. Maybe I'll get back to you."

You mull over the possible existence of karma in an amoral world.

WEEKEND PARENTING

Miranda takes over your bedroom. You sleep on the couch. It is your "every other weekend." Your other two kids are in their 20s and are independent (in every way except financially). You have always been in favor of "independence." You wanted to get away from your own parents as soon as possible. You assume that your kids must want the same. One of the great surprises of your life has been the fact that all three seem to enjoy your company. You live happily in reduced circumstances to support their educations and first steps into the cold, cruel, competitive world.

Miranda is a trip. A curly, red-haired beauty, this 10-year-old is wise beyond her years. She seems to fully understand that you are not a garden-variety dad. She seems okay with it. You are positive that her mother bad-mouths you at every opportunity; however, Miranda is discreet. She is not into stoking any fire between you and your latest ex. When Miranda expresses her concern about your gambling, drinking, or law practice, it is a giveaway that Mom has had her say. You are discreet too. You like pretending that Miranda is your child by some form of male-based parthenogenesis. You do not question her about her mother. You treasure the moments the family court has given you.

On Friday night, the two of you order Thai food to go, and then watch *A Fish Called Wanda* on DVD. You have watched it together at least 10 times. You continually crack each other up with Kevin Kline imitations. "What was that middle part again?" Once Miranda is asleep, you sneak outside and smoke the joint you had set aside to help you couch sleep — not so easy as you age.

It is Saturday morning, and you awake to the clanging sounds of pots and pans — Miranda doing breakfast. Per custom, you will feign sleep while she prepares a breakfast feast. You have taught her, as you did her siblings, to make all the basic breakfasts: eggs (scrambled, fried, poached, boiled, and baked in a frittata); bacon (crisp but never burned); sausage; oatmeal; pancakes, French toast, and waffles; muffins; yogurt/fruit shakes; and fresh-squeezed orange and grapefruit juices. You were teaching life-survival skills. You were also anticipating your own future hangovers. Nothing like a nice, home-cooked breakfast to soothe a headache.

You have no headache but love today's bacon-and-egg scramble with a shake.

"Do you want to go antique shopping today, Mira?"

"No, that's okay, Daddy. Your business is probably a little shaky right now. We don't need to spend any money."

"I don't know where you get this stuff." You obviously know full well. "Let's blow some bucks on some cool, old junk!"

"Daddy, let's take a hike somewhere instead."

Chastened and somewhat humiliated by your daughter's sensible charity, you Mapquest a trail up a scenic hillside. Decked out in many-pocketed shorts and hiking boots, you take your girl walking. It turns out to be fun. More fun than antiques. Miranda was right — as usual.

Back home and tired, Miranda suggests a second breakfast. You make blueberry pancakes and sit down with her to watch *Monty Python and the Holy Grail*. Miranda falls asleep as you read aloud a story by Roald Dahl.

There are times like this when your life seems satisfying. But you know that it is an illusion. Doing "the right thing" is pretty easy with a lovable 10-year-old. What about the rest of it? You have some work to do — mostly on yourself. You are not sure if you are up for that.

WHO'S ZOOMIN' WHOM?

Your first encounter with the polygraph expert is in her office. Margo Duncan is a hard-boiled, dyed blonde in her 60s. She looks as though she has heard and seen it all. Given her profession, she probably has.

She looks you up and down. "Aren't you a cool drink of water! What can I do for you?"

You decide to wade in slowly. "Have you been in this lie-detector business for long, Ms. Duncan?"

"Call me Margo. Thirty years. I'm the best in the city. You would have heard that from the people who sent you, right?"

"I was told that you were very good. I had a double frappuccino at Starbucks this morning. True or false?"

"We can hook you up and find out for sure. But my bet is that you are not the frappuccino type. Stop screwing around with me. What is it you are trying to find out?" So much for getting acquainted.

"My client is a psychologist. He is being sued by a former patient who claims he had sex with her."

"You can sue people for that?"

"California. Brave new world."

"Who am I going to test with the polygraph?"

"My client swears that he did not have sex with the patient." Not even in the Bill Clinton sense of the phrase, you think. "He says that he never touched her inappropriately. I want you to tell me whether he is telling the truth."

"Easy enough," says Margo.

"I don't know if it makes any difference to you, but the consensus is that my client is lying. I would most likely use your findings to confront

73

him and help him make the right decisions. If he is telling the truth, I may also find some use for the results."

Margo considers for a moment. "It doesn't matter to me how you use what I give you. As you can imagine, my results are sometimes not what people are hoping to receive. I assume that a lot of what I do goes into a wastebasket or paper shredder. That is also why I get paid up front — before the disappointment occurs."

"How confident can we be in the polygraph?"

"Few people can fool an experienced operator. Psychotics and psychopaths make our work less than 100 percent reliable. If you literally have no conscience, you can confuse the results. For the vast majority of people, there is no doubt. If my findings are unclear, I will tell you. If I am certain in my assessment, I will tell you that as well."

You and Margo discuss the specific procedures to be used. She simply needs your questions in a "yes" or "no" format.

You have simple questions:

"Did you tell Loren Patagorkis that you loved her?"

"Did you ever touch Loren's breasts?"

"Did you touch Loren's genitals?"

"Did you have sex with Loren?"

Margo has an examination room stocked with serious-looking electric devices. You will be able to watch and hear the proceedings in an adjacent room, behind a one-way mirror. You set a date and time. You write a check.

On the day of reckoning, you squeeze into the observation room with Kate. She complains about the cramped conditions and bad ventilation. You think the close quarters are fine. You definitely enjoy being this close to your attractive associate. It seems, however, that Kate has read your mind as she adheres to the farthest wall.

You state the obvious. "It's a one way mirror. They can't see us."

"Stay where you are. I just had my hair done. Don't you think this is a gigantic waste of time and money?" You are not so sure.

Margo attaches electrodes and adjusts a rubber tube around Dr. Thomas's chest. He sports a metal clip on a finger. Everything hooks up to a console with lights and meters. Margo asks "baseline" questions and takes notes. The console spills out graphed paper.

Margo keeps her voice even as she gets to the point. "Did you at any time touch the breasts of Loren Patagorkis?"

"No."

"Did you at any time touch the genitals of Ms. Patagorkis?"

"No."

"Did you ever tell Ms. Patagorkis that you loved her?"

"No. Absolutely not."

"Did you ever have sexual relations with Ms. Patagorkis?"

"No."

Kate looks at you and shrugs indifferently. At least she didn't start chanting, "Liar, liar, pants on fire."

You have no idea whether or not the doctor's pants are burning. But you are anxious to hear what Margo has to say. Surprisingly, she is not done questioning Dr. Thomas.

"Have you ever had sex with a patient?"

"No."

"Have you ever forced yourself sexually on a woman?"

"No, I have not."

Who the hell told her to ask those things? This will be interesting.

The next day, you meet with Margo in your office. Kate is present as well. Lawrence brings green tea on a bamboo tray. The teacups are miniature monkeys in the classic "see, hear, and speak no evil" poses. Where in the hell does he find this crap? Lawrence must frequent a different class of garage sale than you. Margo seems oblivious to the irony.

"Your client is telling the truth. There is no doubt about it."

You have come to hate that phrase of certitude. It has become part of the standard lexicon for sports announcers and professional athletes. As in, "Our quarterback is the most awesome clutch player of all time — no doubt about it!" or "Tony has really stepped up his game this year. He's worth every penny of that $17 million contract. No doubt about it!" In other words, people continually assert the absence of doubt over matters of opinion for which doubt should be a given. You should probably lighten up.

Maybe you need a skepticism enema. Margo is delivering good news, no doubt about it.

"Margo, is there any likelihood that another polygraph expert would retest and come to different conclusions?"

"Not if they have been fully trained and certified. The data is extremely compelling."

Kate rolls her eyes and rains on the parade. "So, great. We have inadmissible evidence to contradict the extremely persuasive testimony of Loren Patagorkis and the sketchy practices of our client."

You pick up the telephone and call George Lewis. You tell him that you have been thinking about the impressive deposition given by his client. You further tell him that your client is "having trouble dealing with the facts of his situation. You know what I'm saying, George. The doctor could use a little dose of reality. I was thinking … how about we agree that both of our clients will take a polygraph? We can choose someone with a good reputation. We would also agree that the results would be admissible at trial."

George thinks it is a great idea. Why wouldn't he believe in his client? Everybody else does.

A week goes by before you hear from Lewis again.

"Loren won't take a lie-detector test. She says that she was tortured by machinery when she was young. It was part of some weird cult to which her parents belonged. She says that Dr. Thomas knew all about it and that he is using it against her now."

"George, you know what that means. Don't you?"

"Yeah. She's full of crap. Can you get me 10 grand to go away and cover my expenses?"

This is what passes for success in the world of personal-injury litigation. The rest is paperwork.

A month later, you are walking along a pier in Sausalito. Kate, Miranda, and you wave to a sailboat heading out from its berth. Dr. Thomas waves from the deck.

Kate is philosophic. "We got our ten, Lewis got his, and Dr. Thomas is headed around the world. That's not the worst that could happen, right?"

You share your perspective. "Well, he gave up his psychotherapy practice, but he can now officially have sex with any adult he meets."

Dr. Thomas must have found the lawsuit traumatizing. Or maybe he feels as if he avoided a close call. Whatever.

Kate grabs you by the shoulders and seriously intones, "You have a disturbing world view."

"Tell me about it."

"And you should probably keep it to yourself when you are in a parent role."

Miranda laughs. "I've heard much worse than that, Kate." She runs off to chase a pelican.

You exchange shoves with your paralegal. Per custom, that is as much intimacy as the two of you share.

UP AND DOWN AT THE FAIR

I t is summer. You have no plans whatsoever to travel or the funds to do so. You did purchase two tickets for an upcoming Soundgarden reunion concert. You were in the middle of a drunken internet shopping spree, which also netted a half-dozen collarless shirts in a variety of pastel colors.

You have always honored one summer vacation tradition: A day at the county fair with any of your kids who are still willing to go. Miranda has not become too sophisticated for it yet. Your loyalty to this pageantry of thrill rides, farm animals, and fat food is in large part due to the horse races, which take place at an ancient fairground track in the afternoons. You always find a way to fit in a few races. More to the point, you always get the racing form a day early and have your bets figured out for the full day of onsite racing, plus selected tracks around the country. You have a few hundred dollars squirreled away for emergencies. County-fair horse racing meets your idiosyncratic definition of "emergency."

You only need to keep Miranda distracted for a matter of minutes while you lay down all the bets. Occasional meandering back to the track throughout the day will serve to keep you informed as to how your bets have worked out.

To make matters even easier, Miranda is accompanied by her best friend Jenna. They are at the age where they desperately seek to get clear of parental oversight but are uncomfortable if the father figure (you!) is out of sight for too long. This is more than sufficient for your pony purposes.

Independent of your obsessive sneak gambling, you truly do love the goofy Americana. It is nowhere more in your face than in the gigantic signage gracing the food booths. Multicolored, glistening images of creatively assembled grease, dough, and animal byproducts loom. You admire the

LICUADOS, BURRITOS, TACOS, BIONICOS banner, featuring a buxom Hispanic gal riding what looks like an armadillo with a bandana. The Mac & Cheese-Stuffed Bacon Burger beckons. You are tempted by the County Fair Cinnamon Rolls and the Garlic Twisty Fries. And then you spot it: the Krispy Kreme Burger. A half pound of "premium" ground beef, six strips of "home-cured" bacon, nestled between a sliced glazed doughnut, itself massively proportioned. Anything you now choose to consume will be health food by comparison. You order a modest foot-long corndog and encourage Miranda and Jenna to "go for it." They split deep-fried zucchini, funnel cake, and snow cones.

You lobby for someone to try the Pineapple Upside-Down Cake on a stick. It sounds like something only a contortionist could eat without making a mess. As far as you can tell, there are no takers at all.

There are also exhibit halls loaded with collections of all kinds: lunch boxes, Barbie dolls, Disney figures, and Adlai Stevenson campaign buttons. New-fangled leisure products are hawked by crazed salespeople: demonstrations of cleaning products, vibrating massage units, and juicers.

4-H Club prize-winning pigs, cows, chickens, and ducks stink up the hundreds of stalls. You enjoy pretending to be comfortable amongst all of the shit and straw. You make Miranda and Jenna laugh with your ongoing comparisons of the various animals to the people wandering nearby.

The midway is where it is at when you are a preteen. You purchase long strips of ride tickets and dispense them to the girls. You make sure that all the cell phones are aligned and charged. A fall-back meeting place (the Hall of Mirrors) is agreed upon. Miranda and Jenna line up for the Tilt-AWhirl, and you hustle off to the track.

Your mind is sharply focused. You take the steps two at a time to the track entryway. You shake off the tip-sheet salesmen and the program girl. You scan the TV monitors for off-track updates and proceed quickly to the voucher machine. You convert $300 into a small, paper square with an unreadable code. You slide two machines to your left, insert the square into the self-help betting machine, and efficiently log in your predetermined bets. Your heart is racing — just like a thoroughbred, you smugly think.

You bolt back toward the midway without so much as a glance at the race-track itself.

Miranda and her friend have not missed you. They are sauntering down a long row of carnival barkers. All the games of skill and chance look easy. None are, of course. The stuffed-animal prizes somehow call out to children and adults as if they were valued treasures. They are cheap pieces of shit. But context is everything. You vow to impress the girls by winning some large hunk of fabric with eyes. Forty-four dollars later, you have a garish green frog, wearing a monocle, for your dart-throwing/balloon-busting acumen. You've done worse. Miranda does not seem as pleased with the present as you would have liked. Your little girl is growing up. You'll have to teach her the fine points of parimutuel betting soon.

Time for you to get back to the track and for the girls to head for the Haunted House. You estimate that you have 20 minutes for this break.

Again, your efficiency is a marvel. To the bar for a double Jack Daniels on ice, then down to the rail to catch the next race up close. Standing next to you are two middle-aged women, each holding a beer and sporting a paunch. The closest one has a tattoo on the back of her neck, which looks like a flying marmot. You are not sure.

"It's such a rush when those horses come down the stretch," observes tattoo woman. "My name's Sal. Pickin' any winners, yet?"

"Believe it or not, I haven't checked any of the earlier races. These betting slips in my pocket might be worth enough to put me on easy street."

"What's that?"

"Easy Street?"

"Yeah."

"It's a metaphor, Sal."

"Well, buddy boy, if you been pickin' winners, I can think of some places we can go that would probably be a lot more fun than your meta-what-ever-for or your easy street."

"An enchanting suggestion. I'll keep it in mind."

You and Sal banter suggestively. The horses thunder past. It is a rush. You were close to winning an exacta pick but did come through with the winner across the board. You choose to not disclose your good fortune to

Sal and her friend. When their backs are turned, you hightail it out of there and head back to Miranda.

"Have you been having fun, Daddy?" Miranda smirks at Jenna and mimics drinking from a bottle.

"Miro, you are adorable. Let me smack you."

"Jenna's mother is a schoolteacher. That means she is a mandated child-abuse reporter. You watch it!"

The girls guffaw. You chuckle (barely).

Miranda requests that you share the next ride. She and Jenna head for the Ferris wheel, your least favorite of the classic fair thrills. You have never been comfortable with heights. There is something particularly disconcerting about dangling and rocking while stopped at the top of a Ferris wheel, which you have always secretly feared. Oh, well. You have survived it before.

The carnival-ride operators are a grizzled and grumpy breed. They are all men. Regardless of age, they look like they have endured some hardships in the past. The Ferris wheel is manned by a white-haired fellow with an oddly deferential manner. He speaks softly and makes no eye contact as he seats the riders and secures the metal gates across their laps. You reach the head of the line and assume a seat between Jenna and Miranda. As the operator latches you in, he stares full-on into your eyes.

As you ascend in an arc, you remember. Dr. Wayne LaPlume, a client from 15 years ago. He was facing the full boatload of criminal, civil, and medical-board disciplinary charges for multiple alleged instances of unwarranted and unwanted touching of the private parts of his female patients. The victims were both young and old. Dr. LaPlume carried out his overly attentive exams under the guise of comprehensive medical care.

You had argued on his behalf that he was like a reliable auto mechanic who always checked the oil whenever the hood was up. The doctor lost his license, lost his lawsuits, and went to jail for a while. You have never heard from him again.

"Daddy, you don't look so good."

"I'm okay. Just saw a ghost though."

Miranda makes another drinking motion and laughs.

The Ferris wheel does what Ferris wheels do. You figure that Wayne LaPlume may have found the right employment. Every so often, there must be some good crotch-viewing. You are grateful that your daughter and her friend are both wearing shorts.

The wheel begins the stop-and-reload process. But your carriage does not stop at the bottom. Are you getting a friends-and-family, extra-value ride? Or (as you suspect) are you being tortured by the former Dr. LaPlume? You have been suspended for at least 15 minutes. The girls have become quiet. They sense your discomfiture. You are dizzy. You need to pee. You might puke.

You do not want to embarrass Miranda by screaming or yelling. Just as you are nevertheless about to make a noisy protest, Wayne LaPlume gets replaced by another shifty-looking carney. You look at him with unreserved admiration as he brings your ride to an end.

Shaken and in need of a restroom, you wobble across the midway to your goal. Much relieved and now calm, you emerge into the sunlight. Miranda stands, clutching her frog, Jenna at her side. You smile and approach.

"Found you, dickwad!" It is Sal and her sidekick. They have apparently consumed more beer.

"Nice to see you both again," you feebly offer, edging protectively toward Miranda. "Miro, honey. You and Jenna go grab a couple of churros. I'll be right over."

"I guess you like 'em on the young side," cackles Sal.

You are drawing attention of passersby.

"The least you can do," Sal continues, "is buy us a couple of drinks with all your winnings, you cheap fuck!"

You hasten to Sal's side and thrust two 20s in her pudgy hands. She seems content. So are you. As you turn toward the churro stand, you notice one of the stunned onlookers: The Honorable Beverly DeSantos. This is awkward. She is eating a doughnut burger.

PRETRIAL

I t is certain that the Sutcliffe case is going to trial. While Schiff has continued to demand the insurance-policy limits, you have been authorized to counteroffer that the defense would not seek reimbursement for costs of suit if the case were dismissed. In other words, you are offering zilch. No one associated with the defense believes Lois's story. You sure do not. Schiff is extremely miffed that no money is being offered. He takes it as a personal affront. He informs you that he has never lost a jury trial and that the insurance company — the Golden family — and you will all live to regret your collective intransigence. It's on!

Truth be told, you are not all that confident. Maybe you oversold the defensibility of the case to your clients. Fifteen years is a long time to treat a patient. Day-and-night access to a therapist is not a highly regarded nor common practice. Crazy and perpetually angry as she is, Lois had no history of actually pursuing litigation (just threatening it). Schiff truly does have an impressive track record, and his expert witness is a psychiatrist with lots of experience in trials. Unfortunately, you gave him his first taste of forensic work years ago! There was also the "bad fact" of Dr. Golden marrying a former patient, even though it has not yet been formally acknowledged. If Schiff has the chance, he is going to get that information out of Laura Golden. You have not told a soul.

You have retained two psychologist expert witnesses. Dr. Ussachevsky is a clinical psychologist with an exceptional eye for detail. You have worked with him in the past and have always benefited from his obsessive review of records. He informs you of many subtle but important facts. He has conducted a psychological evaluation of Lois at your request. (The defense is entitled to at least one such exam by a doctor of its choice.) Dr. Martin is also a clinical psychologist. You have retained him specifically for the purpose of testifying about borderline personality disorders. He has reviewed Lois's treatment records and deposition but has never met her in person. Dr. Martin is intellectually combative. You believe that he will get Schiff to foam at the mouth.

Dr. Ussachevsky has provided you with a written report in which he meticulously documents the data supporting the conclusion that Lois suffers from a long-standing, borderline personality disorder. According to the Diagnostic and Statistical Manual of Mental Disorders (DSM), all personality disorders begin in adolescence or early adulthood. They represent pervasive and inflexible ways of experiencing the world and behaving, such that a person with the disorder deviates from cultural expectations and is subject to significant distress and impairment in their functioning. The "essential feature" of a borderline personality disorder is that there is a pervasive pattern of unstable interpersonal relationships. The person with this disorder has disturbing changes in self-image and emotions and acts impulsively. You adamantly refuse to consider how much that description fits you. (And just about everyone else you've ever found remotely interesting.)

The DSM lists nine criteria for diagnosis of borderline personality. Any five of them are sufficient to establish the diagnosis. You have amassed evidence, and Dr. Ussachevsky has sifted through it. Lois has exhibited all or almost all of them:

1. Frantic efforts to avoid real or imagined abandonment.
2. A pattern of unstable interpersonal relationships characterized by alternating between extremes of idealization and devaluation (loving and hating).
3. Unstable self-image or sense of self.
4. Impulsivity in at least two areas that are self-damaging.
5. Recurrent suicidal behavior, gestures, or threats.
6. Marked reactivity of mood (e.g., intense dysphoria, irritability, or anxiety).
7. Chronic feelings of emptiness.
8. Inappropriate intense anger.

9. Transient, stress-related paranoid ideation or severe dissociative symptoms.

The three themes you want to impress on the jury are obvious:

1. Dr. Golden was an ethical, competent, and caring psychiatrist.
2. Ms. Sutcliffe was an extremely difficult patient with a long-standing mental disorder.
3. That disorder, if understood by the jury, explains why the lawsuit is being pursued, despite its lack of merit.

Years ago, you learned that a defense attorney has to do more at trial than act defensively. Trial for the defense is more than just parrying the thrusts of the plaintiff. A defense attorney needs to actively provide an explanation as to why the lawsuit has been brought and why the plaintiff is mistaken in seeking money from your client. Simply accusing the plaintiff of lying is a weak defense. Accusing the plaintiff of lying for money is not much better. It is far preferable to put on evidence that helps the jury understand the kind of people the parties are and what kind of lives they have led. Show how a mental disorder interacts with the plaintiff's history to bring about a distortion of the truth, and you've got something.

You feel no animosity for Lois Sutcliffe. You are certain that her accusations against your client are false, but you can still feel sympathy for her circumstances. She does not deserve money nor does her asshole attorney. You sometimes have a quaint belief in juries and tell yourself that your next one can dispassionately judge this case on its merits. You will get your defense verdict without having to demolish Lois's character. (Sure.)

You just want to take full advantage of her mental disorder. It is not her fault that she is so screwed up.

In preparation for trial, you meet with Laura and Adam. You explain that you want the jury to see Laura attend the proceedings once in a while. You will be making the decision about her testifying as trial progresses. You will coordinate the appearances with Adam. Laura need not wear black, but she should be dressed modestly. Neither one should act upset or animated.

You have a "suite" at the Hotel Sparta in downtown San Jose. This probably is not the kind of place in which most out-of-town trial attorneys stay. This is not the kind of place most people with full-time jobs stay. But your credit card has a slim remaining limit, and you want to be close to the courthouse. Courts often are in somewhat funky urban areas. Silicon Valley has not spread the upscale glamour to all of the San Jose civic buildings.

On the bright side, there is a "concierge" named Manny, who informs you on the first day that he is available to find you "whatever you need, pal." Your mind boggles at that offer. You focus. You have a lot of work to do. You organize your 20 Bekins' boxes of documents and check your briefcase for pens, legal pads, markers, Post-its, and Breath Savers. The suite is not much smaller than your apartment, so you feel none of that hotel claustrophobia. In fact, the bathroom facilities are far superior to your crib. You admire the brass fixtures and the well-aligned towels (even though they are a bit gray and worn). No minibar, but that is a good thing. In the past, you have had accounting problems at checkout for little bottles of liquor and Snickers. The pay TV promises adult programming as well as a bounty of first-run movie choices. Again, you need to remind yourself not to repeat past mistakes of judgment related to channel flipping through pay-per-view selections. You are going to be one disciplined motherfucker.

The only readily apparent downside of your lodging is the odor. You can't tell exactly what it is, but it seems to most pungently attach to the sofa and the side chair. It is vaguely familiar. Alfalfa? Crotch? Have farmers from Iowa been screwing on the furniture? You vow to clear your mind of this question. Next thing you know, you will be perusing the adult titles for rural-based porn. Focus, focus, focus. You have read all the reports, records, depositions, pleadings, and psychology texts and articles cited by the experts. You have prepared briefs and witness questions. You are a trial machine. You are also a loner in a cheap hotel, getting ready to fight for a cause that no one probably cares about as much as you. Focus.

A trial judge once told you that trial was like going on a submarine mission. The outside world gets blocked out, and your attention is devoted entirely to your job. It's not always like that for you. You might still want to check out the pay-per-view and possibly have some conversations with Manny. Still, this is the time when other obligations take a back seat. You are, in your way, psyched.

TRIAL DAY ONE

Before a jury panel is assembled, attorneys typically meet with the judge and go through pretrial motions and a bunch of housekeeping concerns. This judge is a piece of work. He is what you think people mean when they describe someone as "craggy." Old and tough, he probably stormed Iwo Jima. No smiles. No personal comments. He just wants you to present your argument, and then shut up and sit down.

Judge Gunderson is a former district attorney. He has been on the bench for 22 years. The judge is definitely "old school." There was a time when almost all superior court judges were like him: white, upper class, and politically conservative. California has been on the vanguard, as in many things, by appointing judges with diverse backgrounds. In fact, Judge Gunderson would be an unlikely candidate for the job nowadays. He could retire at any time with a generous pension. He must love his work. He might be a little bit of a sadist like many of his peers. You are fine with that, so long as he gets his jollies by torturing your opponent as much or more than you. He seems to have little patience for Schiff and his theatrical style. Repeatedly, the judge tells Schiff that he has heard enough of his talking. Two times, he cautions Schiff that any further argument will be considered "contempt." You are falling in love.

One of your motions is to set limits on the examination of Mrs. Golden.

You point out that the widow has already suffered mightily by virtue of this lawsuit and that Schiff has demonstrated a disregard for propriety in his deposition of Mrs. Golden. You request that Schiff be prohibited from any questions that are not specifically directed to the widow's knowledge of Ms. Sutcliffe. The judge says that he will not rule on your request until Ms. Golden takes the stand. You do not mind waiting for that. Schiff has not served Laura with a subpoena to appear because she is on your witness list, but that in no way obligates you to call her. You are one cagey son of a gun. If you do not call Laura to testify, Schiff can do so — if his people can find her to serve with a subpoena. You plan on her disappearance during trial.

You finish the day with the judge's rulings, a list of potential jurors, and an earful of instructions from the judge as to how you and opposing counsel are to conduct yourselves over the next two weeks.

You return to Hotel Sparta to study your files. You call Miranda and get ready for the submarine voyage. You recall the movie *Das Boot*. If you are not mistaken, the weeks on board the submarine are alternately pleasant and terrifying, but the crew makes it back to port safely. When the welcoming ceremony and back-patting begin, the Allied planes appear and make mincemeat of everyone. Food for thought.

TRIAL DAY TWO

L ike every trial attorney, you use the jury-selection process to start shamelessly ingratiating yourself and to preview your case. The avowed purpose of *voir dire* is to question potential jurors and weed out bias and prejudice. If that was really the only purpose, the attorneys for both sides would never take part. You (and your opposing counsel) could care less about a little bias and prejudice as long as it favors your client. In fact, one way to describe jury selection is a contest between attorneys to see who is more successful at getting a head start in ingratiating himself or herself with the umpires.

In an ideal world, the jurors would be intelligent people with a commitment to serve the community. You are always disappointed when the folks take their seats in the jury box to be questioned. Some are extremely smart. They almost universally are bright enough to figure out a way to get out of having to serve. The ones who offer no excuse are challenged by your opponent. He wants the sullen, intellectually challenged types. He wants the people who work for the post office.

In this trial, the judge is allowing very little time for attorney questions. Judges can be arbitrary about such things in civil trials. Fine by you. You politely ask everyone a few questions about their jobs or families. You ask if they can be fair to a deceased defendant. You ask if they accept the notion that people can make false claims as a result of mental illness. You exercise your challenges on people who look angry and anyone who relates a bad experience with a physician or psychotherapist. In fact, you would rather minimize the number of jurors who know anything about the way psychotherapy works. You would prefer jurors who think that anyone who goes to a psychiatrist must be pretty darn screwed up!

You make a point of taking notes as to what jurors say about their lives, but you actually don't care too much. You keep track of their names as they take their seats in the jury box. You look attentive when they speak. You nod and smile obsequiously. But you do not share the prevailing view that trials are won or lost at the jury-selection phase.

Some lawyers bring jury consultants to trial. They rely on supposed expertise of social scientists to help with jury challenges. You are skeptical as to the value of that assistance. The truth is that you are bored with this process and can't wait to get started with witnesses on the stand.

Schiff performs his usual over-the-top act. "Ladies and gentlemen, if selected for this jury, you will learn of shockingly exploitive and perverted acts by a physician in a position of power and trust. Do any of you think that you will be unable to listen attentively to such matters?"

You stand and quietly observe. "Sounds a bit argumentative to me, Judge."

"Is that an objection, counsel?" the annoyed judge responds.

"It most certainly is, Your Honor."

"Sustained. Next time I expect to hear your objection made in the proper form."

You have been chastised but realize that this trial is going to be by the book. You vow to be the "good attorney" who does what the judge wants. Schiff could not play that role even if he wanted to, which he does not.

"Judge," Schiff explains, "I need to warn the potential jurors of the raw, sexual enslavement suffered by my client so that people who are too sensitive can so inform us."

"No. You have no such need. Jurors will make up their own minds based on evidence and my instructions of the law. One more statement like that and I will consider a mistrial."

Schiff is quieted for the moment. But similar exchanges go on for the rest of the day. You have to admire Schiff at some level. He just does not give a damn whether or not the judge hates him. And this is the *beginning* of trial!

By 5 p.m., a jury has been selected. Things will get rolling tomorrow.

Back in your somewhat smelly room, you review your notes on the jurors. You will not spend much more time thinking about them as individuals. You are unlikely to remember anyone's name by the end of trial. Your case will ultimately be decided by this mix of young and old women and men with varying successes in life. One obvious stoner. One old guy who seems to be on the verge of dementia. A woman who reminds you of an ex-wife. The usual.

TRIAL DAY THREE

Schiff appears with two assistants. They are in their 20s, one male and one female. They scurry in response to Schiff's commands. They both appear to be traumatized. No wonder. The young woman seems to be tasked with locating documents and facts; the man fiddles constantly with audiovisual equipment.

You are flying solo. Your preference is to be The Lone Ranger. That classic hero from your youth wasn't actually alone: He had Tonto. Maybe the moniker reflected his existential angst. You can certainly relate. You do not like to appear as if you need a crew to help you with the "simple" job of presenting Dr. Golden's defense. Starting tomorrow, Kate is going to be in court to watch some of the proceedings. The insurance company will have someone monitoring trial off and on. Adam Golden has said that he will accompany Laura whenever you think her presence will be helpful. But you will always sit at counsels' table alone — you and your dead Tonto, Dr. Golden.

Schiff's opening statement is long. You have determined that you will not object, interrupt, or make faces. Instead, you almost fall asleep. He informs the jury that Ms. Sutcliffe is in such a fragile psychological state (thanks to Dr. Golden) and will only be allowed by her current psychiatrist to attend trial when testifying. Good one, Schiff! He probably cannot stand too much time in his client's presence any more than other people can. In any event, he will have an absentee client for much of trial too.

Your opening statement is professorial. You continue with your two themes:

1. Dr. Golden was a dedicated and caring psychiatrist who demonstrated remarkable patience with a difficult client.

2. Lois Sutcliffe has a borderline personality disorder that fully explains her need to tear down the doctor she once relied on and loved.

You promise that the evidence will establish these facts. You have a large, blown-up graphic of the DSM page, which lists the nine criteria for borderline personality disorder. You point to it continually, like a TV weather guy and his map. You plan to drag out this exhibit every chance you get.

Schiff calls his first witness: Dr. Victor Hector. You know this guy well. He hates your guts, and you return the sentiment. Many years before this case, Dr. Hector testified on behalf of one of your clients who was suing an insurance company for bad-faith claims practices. Dr. Hector was the treating psychiatrist. When you met with him to prepare for trial, he told you that he had never given testimony in trial. He told you that he would "say whatever you wanted." You had explained that it did not work quite that way. You were not there to tell him what to say, only to help him find the best way to say it. Things had gone downhill quickly from that point. Never had you encountered such a clueless whore. He undoubtedly thought that you were a clueless pimp.

Over the years, Dr. Hector developed a reputation as a very active forensic expert. No wonder, since he continued, in your humble opinion, to say anything the attorney hiring him wanted said. Your encounters in depositions and trials had been contentious. They were also tedious because Hector had learned that, when you get paid several hundred dollars an hour, you can make a lot of money by nonstop talking. His answers to questions in deposition were the stuff of legend. He could answer the simplest question — "What was your diagnosis of the plaintiff's disorder?" — with a 30-minute, self-serving exposition. He and Schiff were a match made in heaven for court reporters, who also get financial benefit from verbosity. They charge by the page.

Schiff begins his direct examination of Hector at about 1 p.m. Four hours later, we have learned all about the doctor's fantastic training and professional accomplishments and have just started to hear about his review of records and evaluation of Ms. Sutcliffe. You have a slim hope that you may begin your cross-examination sometime tomorrow.

You have already started to bond with the bailiff, who is a red-faced and balding senior citizen with the boiler of a man in a long-time sedentary job. He wears a sheriff's uniform and carries a sidearm. His job duties appear to be typical: Keep the water pitchers filled, tell people to "all rise" when the judge enters the courtroom, and frown at people who talk when court is in session. You also have seen him tell a couple of young men in the jury pool to remove their caps. That's about it. But you know that his real purpose is to leap into action to protect and serve the court personnel when violence threatens, which it never does and almost certainly never will.

As far as your personal safety is concerned, you have always assumed that lawyers are pretty far down the list of people for whom a bailiff might take a bullet. Bailiffs usually view lawyers with disdain. But you nevertheless seem to get along well with them over the course of trials. Maybe it is because you share their disdain for your profession. Let's face it. You have generalized disdain for law-enforcement professionals too. You have your reasons. But you like this guy. The two of you have exchanged subtle eye raising while Dr. Hector testified. You wish that all cops were more like he was.

You have never been convicted of a crime but have spent a little time in jail. The first time you were arrested, you were 22 years old. You were on a summer road trip with two law-school friends. Do young adults even take "road trips" anymore? The age of majority was still cause for wonder and delight, and your fresh-faced trio was thrilled to enter questionable-looking bars and clubs and served large quantities of alcohol, usually without displaying your IDs. In Burley, Idaho, you overdid it. This was to become your custom. You were instructed, in very clear terms, to exit the premises of what had seemed to be a friendly cowboy bar. Your traveling companion Rueben had complained about the "shitty white-trash music" on the jukebox. He complained loudly and urgently as if the heavily muscled bartender with a crew cut was going to drop everything and search out some good rhythm and blues.

By the time you and your other traveling companion Tony had hustled Rueben to a corner booth, the three of you were on cowboy-bar probation. Not having yet honed your ability to consume massive quantities of intoxicants while negotiating tricky social situations, you had attempted to engage in flirtatious banter with four middle-aged ladies in an adjacent booth. Your recollection of your specific conversation starters is limited to the request that "You girls should let me squeeze in there. I am young and eager to learn!" The women actually seemed to find you amusing. Their dates, who were nearby playing foosball, did not. Does anyone over 30 still play foosball?

Outside on the empty street, the three of you play-acted gun-fighting duels. Instead of guns, you used half-empty (half-filled) bottles of beer. Burley's finest interrupted the fun and escorted you to the police station. They mocked you pretty good. After about an hour in a holding cell, you three *caballeros* were brought before a crisp and bright-eyed sergeant, who was seated behind a tiny, cheap-looking desk. The sergeant was tall and lean and wore his 20-gallon hat, making him look even more like a figure of outsized authority.

"You would probably be surprised to find out how long we can keep you in jail. But the fact is that we don't care for your company all that much. Do you have accommodations elsewhere for what remains of tonight?"

You all assured him that you did: Ramada Inn, near the interstate.

"If you promise me that you are on that interstate before noon tomorrow, we'll give you a ride back to your hotel. And I don't ever want to see you in my town again. Agreed?"

You bet it was. And yet, you always feel that this was not a truly charitable deal. You never have been able to place it, but you believe that the sergeant was re-enacting a scene from some John Wayne movie. He got some ego stroke out of it. You got grateful humiliation. You are still irked when you think of all the slick retorts you could have made. Nevertheless, you are never going back to Burley.

Trial Day Three

Returned to the Sparta, you and Manny discuss games of chance and the availability of same within a reasonable distance. There is an "Indian casino" in town. Manny will be getting you some printed literature. In your room, you postulate that there must be a developmental explanation for always being on the verge of misbehavior. Damned if you can get any more introspective than that! You put on your PJ bottoms and Steely Dan T-shirt. You have two of them. You sing *Show Biz Kids* to yourself. This is the same way you dress when at home and in for the evening. If you stayed in your bungalow, there would be no issue. But you have multiple reasons to wander into the common areas — laundry and garbage cans — and retrieve stuff from your car. You know that you are a funky, middle-aged man, publicly displaying yourself in PJs and vintage-rock (jazz) shirts. Regardless, you think that no one will notice. You are becoming senile. This is the proof.

TRIAL DAY FOUR

Dr. Hector's testimony continues. He and Schiff pick up the pace a bit. As much as they both love to hear themselves talk, they also know at some level that they should try to keep the jury awake.

Hector's opinions boil down to this: Ms. Sutcliffe definitely did *not* suffer from any personality disorder or any chronic psychological condition prior to seeing Dr. Golden. Her difficulties were of a type frequently encountered as a matter of course in transitioning from school to the work force. Lois was bright and motivated and — but for Dr. Golden — would have eventually become a lawyer with a six-figure income. Her lack of social relationships was due to the demands placed on her by Dr. Golden. His use of her for sexual and emotional gratification was consistent with the actions of therapists who fail to maintain strict boundaries. The fact that Dr. Golden took Lois's calls day and night proved, to Dr. Hector's satisfaction, that the relationship was not professional.

"It may seem as though Dr. Golden was being a kind and caring person. In fact, he was enabling and reinforcing dependency!" Dr. Hector exclaimed.

Finally — and somewhat shockingly since Dr. Hector had not expressed this in deposition — he testifies that Dr. Golden had been subtly encouraging Ms. Sutcliffe to kill herself. He did so by "allowing" her to stockpile potentially lethal amounts of medication.

Kate is in attendance. You glance at her as you walk to the lectern to begin your questioning. Dr. Hector stares at you. He has beady eyes and a poor hair dye job. (Why do men with means go in for those? Your mother did much better with her own Miss Clairol kits.) You assume that Dr. Hector paid someone for that mess. The jet-blue/black hair makes a particularly bad match with the pasty complexion. His heavy jowls weigh down the other facial features, which may at one time have been somewhat hand-some. He is smug as hell. He can't wait for you to begin. You tell yourself to be patient and go slowly.

You pick up a copy of Dr. Hector's voluminous CV from which you have removed the heavy staple. As you approach the witness stand, you "accidentally" drop the pages onto the floor and kick them around a bit with your foot as if trying to encourage them to reassemble.

"Well, Doctor. I think we've all heard enough about your background. Let's get down to your opinions concerning Ms. Sutcliffe."

Dr. Hector has no sense of humor, but the jury does. At least half the jurors are openly smirking.

You perp march Dr. Hector through the DSM criteria for borderline personality disorder. You get him to admit that these are the psychiatric profession's agreed-upon standards. You are pleased that he and Schiff have decided to dispute the applicability of the diagnosis to Lois. Hector assures you (and the jury) that the diagnosis "doesn't fit" poor Ms. Sutcliffe. You dramatically gesticulate toward your DSM blow up with each question you ask.

"Doctor, isn't it true that Ms. Sutcliffe became frantic when she learned of the death of Dr. Golden?"

"I don't know that 'frantic' is the right word."

"Wasn't she 'frantic' at being abandoned?"

"No more than any patient who has been infantilized and exploited by her doctor for 15 years."

"Most patients without personality disorders make multiple suicide attempts when their psychiatrist dies?"

"If the doctor has so cruelly abused them, they do."

"Isn't it true that Ms. Sutcliffe had a history of idealizing her healthcare providers and then hating them?"

"There is nothing out of the ordinary in that either."

"Didn't Ms. Sutcliffe complain of chronic feelings of emptiness over the course of many years?"

"That's a very subjective notion."

"It's in the DSM, is it not? It's in her treatment records for years before she ever met Dr. Golden, is it not?"

"It really is vague and certainly not sufficient in and of itself to support a borderline diagnosis."

"Doctor, would you at least admit that Ms. Sutcliffe was recurrently suicidal in thoughts and behavior?"

"Only in the remote past and more recently because of the trauma caused by Dr. Golden."

This song and dance goes on for a couple of hours. Hector is definitely sweating. The jury is definitely enjoying his discomfiture. (You sure are.) The judge recesses trial until tomorrow. You glance at Kate. She is wide-eyed and maybe even excited. You like that look.

You pack up your briefcase. The courtroom has emptied as you and Kate exit.

She grabs your arm and whispers, "You were great."

In the parking lot, you say, "I'm just around the corner at the beautiful Hotel Sparta. Do you want to give me your feedback over a drink?"

"Do they have a bar?"

"Not exactly. But I can get anything — and I do mean *anything* — you want delivered to my suite." You consciously refer to a "suite" to make the surroundings seem a little more upscale. You know in your dark heart that Kate is thinking the same thing as you.

You do not wait for room service. It has been a year or more since you have had this particular kind of fun. The funk of your room bears new aromas. Sweat — yours and hers. Her fragrance is something close to cinnamon and lilac. You happily drown in whatever it is. Your parietal lobe is having a fiesta. It had been wondering whether there was ever again going to be anything other than parties for one. You haven't forgotten how to ride a bike. This is a very nice bike.

Your conversation is minimal but functional.

"Could you loosen that a little?"

"There … yes, there."

"Lift up a little."

"Oh, more of that!"

"Don't stop! Don't stop!"

"Can you bring me a towel?"

Lots of oxygen consumption, exchange of bodily fluids, tactile stimulation, and nature's unfolding and enfolding.

You are transported. You are satiated. You fall asleep without reviewing your notes for tomorrow.

You awaken with a smile on your face. It's probably the same one you had when you fell asleep. There is no one else here. There is a croissant and a paper cup of lukewarm coffee next to the bed.

A note: "That was a mistake. It was a pleasant mistake, but I cannot keep working with you if you have any illusion that it might happen again. Go get 'em today, Tiger. Kate"

That is a matter-of-fact message. You appreciate the regret and the determination to avoid a repeat performance. Was there something the tiniest bit implicit in that note, as in, "it could be repeated under the right circumstances"? Kate had not absolutely dismissed that possibility. You make a mental note to pursue that line of inquiry in the indefinite future. (Perchance to dream.)

How could something so pleasurable have been a "mistake"? Why would your work life have to change just because of yesterday evening's interlude? You wonder whether you think too much or not enough. It occurs to you that this question answers itself.

TRIAL DAY FIVE

Testimony from Lois's family, who have flown out from the East Coast. They are a homely bunch. Mom, Dad, and brother Michael are put through their paces by Schiff. They all agree: Lois was a precocious child and an excellent student. Her promising future was unexpectedly derailed by some minor mental problems (and resulting mental hospitalizations). Her move to California was a surprise to all. They had lost close contact ever since. They knew, however, that "something was wrong" out here in the West. They were not at all surprised to learn that Lois had been subjected to mistreatment by someone here.

"Why else would she have languished as she did in marginal jobs and no social life?" says Mom.

You do not have the heart to suggest that they are in denial of the rather obvious fact that Lois is CRAZY.

The psychiatrist who "discovered" Lois's abuse is next. You, of course, try to help him see the error of his ways.

Dr. Runge is very proud of himself for having cracked the mystery of Ms. Sutcliffe's suicidality in response to Dr. Golden's death. You pound him with all of the things he doesn't know about Ms. Sutcliffe's history. As the cross-exam continues, it becomes more and more obvious that Dr. Runge is the person who put the idea of a potential legal action in Lois's head. Not only did he initiate the conversation about possible unethical behavior by Dr. Golden, he provided Lois with a pamphlet, which set out a patient's legal rights in response to psychotherapist/patient sex. Dr. Runge's motivations were almost certainly honorable, but he is almost unbearably naive. (Or so you hope the jury believes as they head out the door.)

That's it for this week of trial. When you resume on Monday, Lois will be testifying at last. Your witnesses will take the stand. You hunker down at the Sparta and work through Friday evening. Kate's visit seems to have had a good effect. You stay away from pay-per-view.

You check in with Miranda. "Yo, Miro. I am living the high life down in San Jose. I wish you could be here."

"Are you in a casino?"

"No, darling. You've been listening to your mother again. Remember I told you about this trial in which my client died?"

"That doesn't sound fair. It seems like he has suffered enough."

"I couldn't agree with you more. I can't wait for you to go to law school so you can help me with this stuff."

"That's about as likely as you winning at craps tonight."

"I told you not to listen to ... oh, never mind. Love you, little girl."

"Love you too, Daddy."

You imagine Mira's mother being forced at gunpoint to attend a Quaker prayer meeting — in purgatorial infinity.

You open the hotel room curtains, which you have kept closed all week. You stare at the busy San Jose city street. The sun has set, and the car headlights are on. Even though you are six floors up, there is an almost audible buzz emanating from the restaurants and bars lining the street in both directions. The sound is probably all in your head, but you certainly know the world that is getting in motion below.

People are pouring into those eating and drinking establishments. They are meeting, talking, exchanging phone numbers and vital statistics, making plans. Later tonight, there will be romance and imitations of it. Some people will be robbed in this city. Purses, wallets, and hearts. Maybe one or two citizens will be killed. Every expectation is shadowed by a potential regret.

You unwrap a PowerBar and feel ambivalence about the safety of your suite cocoon. Just before you drop off, you think that you should be out there and in danger.

The harsh light of Saturday intrudes like a bugle call. Even under normal circumstances, bachelor weekends can be tough. You are struck by what you consider a profound insight: Your recent love fest with Kate is the equivalent of the "boundary crossings" that make up the bulk of your practice.

Everything was surely "consensual," and there were no undue influences, drugs, drunkenness, or quid pro quo. But there sure as hell was a lot of "transference' and "countertransference." You have changed (probably forever) the structure of a professional relationship with someone who clearly trusted you and held you in high regard. You have those same feelings for her, but the difference is that you are the boss. It was up to you to keep your interactions uncluttered. Your innocent and honorable intentions are meaningless. In truth, there is absolutely no way the two of you can successfully pretend it never happened. (Shit.)

No wonder your life has run such a ragged course. Time and again, people have praised your talents and abilities. Time and again, you disappoint with gaudy self-destruction. You know that you sometimes miss the "big picture." You sometimes are inattentive to details. In your personal life, as in work, you are essentially a fuck-up with skills.

What happens next? You try to put the distractions of your life out of your head. Down periscope. Run silent, run deep.

KNOW THYSELF

Maybe it was not such a great idea to stay at the Sparta over the weekend. Manny is off duty. His replacement is a wrinkly old guy who doesn't tell you his name even though you give him yours.

The Bekins boxes stacked across your hotel room wall now look like the catacombs. Despite your best intentions to review and analyze, these files are now just a bunch of crumbling bone and cartilage. They are off-putting, to say the least.

Focus. You have options. Pay-per-view. Stroll around the town. Call friends who will all be busy doing Saturday-night activities. See if wrinkly man in the lobby plays cards. Eat a couple of PowerBars and hit the sack early. They say that everything looks better in the morning. You believe that this room is actually going to look more depressing in the Sunday morning light, but you will give it a try.

As you wind down, you watch a travel-channel documentary about Mexico. You wonder if it will feature headless victims of drug cartels. No, it is more conventional fare. There is an exciting sequence on the Acapulco cliff divers. You recall having witnessed the somewhat less dramatic cliff divers at the edges of Mazatlan. Those young men dove into the Pacific bay with jagged rock formations jutting upward like the devil's skewers. As in Acapulco, the divers wait until a compatriot on shore signals that the tourists have ponied up a sufficient payment for the leap (usually 100 pesos). You had understood the brilliant marketing. People are induced to pay in advance for an expected thrill that carried the possibility of injury or death.

The diver embraces the sky and plummets. Every observer holds their breath. In each private heart resides anticipation … regret? … relief. Talk about getting your money's worth! At the end of the day, do your clients

— especially the ones who have crossed boundaries with patients — ultimately get what they bargained for? (Do you?)

As you lie in bed, belly nicely stuffed, you mentally replay your own psychotherapist experiences. When marriage #2 started to hit the skids, you agreed to go to couples' counseling with Leann Lecroix, PhD. You have now come to the conclusion that, once a married couple seeks counseling, the die is already cast. The therapy becomes a way to more painfully act out the dissolution. But you were innocent then.

You did hope for the aid and wisdom of Dr. Lecroix. She was a large-boned woman, 10 years older than you. Annie (as she let you know you should call her) was also brash and dynamic, and not at all shy about giving specific directions to you and your wife.

"Never go to bed angry. Have sex at least every other night. Let yourselves go. Be creative. And, most importantly, come here on Wednesday so we can sort it all out."

The Wednesday expanded into two additional sessions, one with you and one with your wife Clarissa. In addition, Annie "highly recommended" that you and Clarissa participate in a couples' group therapy session every Friday evening. This was as close as you have ever come to being a member of a cult. (It was a cult.)

You and Clarissa (and two other miserable couples) met to dissect your respective weeks of conflict and dysfunction. Annie presided with advice, criticism, instruction, and (occasional) praise. You acolytes argued with each other's spouses in addition to your own. Sometimes you left the group, taking comfort that maybe your marriage was not as bad as one of the other couple's. More often, you thought that yours took first prize for being fucked up.

The cult of Annie was of absolutely no benefit to your marital difficulties. It did, however, make explicit the things that you and Clarissa hated about each other. It also provided the opportunity for Annie to suggest that you might be happier exploring the joys of a personal relationship with her.

The power of transference is easy to dismiss. But practically everyone has, at some time, had a crush on an authority figure upon whom they project idealized characteristics. You have been under the spell of female teachers off and on since the second grade. Completely ordinary therapists are transformed into beloved avatars by their patients. You fell for Annie. Secretly, the two of you made plans to spend a weekend away.

Annie then revealed them to Clarissa. "You need to truly see how far apart you two have drifted." (No wonder you are gun-shy about women and therapists.)

You subsequently have seen some individual therapists. The last one was a disciple of Albert Ellis, the "inventor" of rational emotive therapy (RET). This treatment was based on the premise that a patient should be confronted with the illogic of his or her thinking and cognitively retrained to confront life's problems with sense rather than sensation. You had tired of California's get-in-touch-with-your-emotions crap. You embraced the East Coast disciplined thinking (represented by RET), which would lead to well-considered, directed action to clear away the soupy detritus of your conscious decision-making. The unconscious be damned!

After four months of RET with the RET disciple, which you eagerly glommed, you awoke one night and could not return to sleep. Heart pounding, you began analyzing as you had been doing of late. The pace of your brain was frenetic.

"Spending this last Thanksgiving alone could be seen as a metaphor for a divestiture of my past so-called 'connections' and a harbinger of a lean and spare life to come, stripped of illusory and mostly mythic memory and false affiliations, since, as I know full well, I am essentially ... no! in *reality* ... alone in this life and must make my own way without hopeful reliance on those who, for quite legitimate reasons of their own, hold their personal needs and survival paramount to mine, and so, the *feelings* of loneliness I *think* I experience are in fact the manifestation of my finally realized state of private ownership of my interior world, and, if I could jettison tradition and false/exaggerated attachment to individuals previously endorsed as 'family' and 'friends,' I might psychologically shift forward to embrace a life of clear-eyed realism. To wit, I am entirely alone. Make the most of it."

You stared at the dark ceiling for hours. At 6 a.m., you picked up the phone and canceled your next 100 therapy appointments. You decided that you much preferred self-delusion. Even bleak loneliness is better than over-dosing on rational analysis.

On Sunday morning, you decide to check out the local casino with Manny's promotional literature in hand.

The Startrax Casino is, of course, open 24 hours, seven days a week. The Startrax Indians were probably a hard-working tribe. Who goes to these places at 8 a.m. on a Sunday morning? (You and about 50 or 60 Asians.) You spot a couple of brothers at the poker tables, but otherwise this might as well be Macau.

Your first and second wives enjoyed gambling as much as you. (Not a good thing.) After much soul searching and "encouragement" at the severe hands of wife #3, you have adapted some guidelines to gaming:

- Give yourself a strict time limit at the tables.
- Do not take any credit or debit cards into the casino.
- The folding money on your person is your limit.

Okay. You are out of here by 10 a.m. You have $400 in your wallet. There is another $200 in your shoe. Enjoy yourself. You like blackjack. No, it is something more than that. You ease yourself onto the blackjack table stool as if it were a warm bath. You feel embraced by the dealer and your fellow gamblers in a nonphysical hug. This is home. You make every play according to the odds. You are not a card counter, but you play as a professional would. There is no playing of hunches. You play a statistically correct game. It does not matter if other players or the dealer are sociable. You interact with others if they seem so inclined, but you "hit," "stay," "double down," and split pairs in exactly the same way, depending on the dealer's up card. Most of the other players are not sociable. All of the young Asian men seem to have Asperger's syndrome. They make no eye contact and manage only the barest responses to questions. The women are sometimes talkative but look as if they are well kept. (Large diamond rings and large bets.)

You are making $20, $30, and $40 bets. You do not double down on 10 unless the dealer shows less than a nine. In other words, you are betting conservatively. After an hour, you are ahead $200. An hour to go, and you press it a bit. You bet $100 every other deal. You get ahead $700. You should leave now. No way. There are 30 minutes left on your time limit.

A new player takes the chair to your right. He immediately starts playing stupidly. He takes hits that will likely bust and stays on hands that anyone with a brain would hit. Is he a "cooler"? You cannot imagine that the casino management would bother to fuck up your game with such smallfry winnings. Yet, this is textbook disruptive. Your winnings plummet.

You lose all of the house money and dip into your original stake. Your selfimposed time limit is up. It is definitely time to leave, but you can't do it. You know better. You foresee exactly where things are headed. (You *really* know better.)

You soldier on. The experience of being hundreds of dollars ahead only moments ago is still raging through your brain. Your serotonin levels have spiked and crashed. You must regain something back. Winning or losing are almost equally acceptable alternatives. Slinking away a few dollars ahead or behind is not an option. That is for wimps. (Or for people whose brain chemistry is more balanced.) To you, the in-betweens of life seem to negate existence.

You blow through the $400. You slip off your shoe and pull out the last $200 bills. There is no way to do this subtly while sitting at a blackjack table. You could have gone to the restroom and been discreet, but you do not care. (Take these foot-stink bills!)

You receive your two $100 chips and place them on the bet circle. You face your fate with a straight face and sweaty palms. You are dealt a nine and a queen. The dealer shows a six. Of course you stay pat. The odds are very much in favor of a dealer bust. He turns over the hole card: a five. The jack that follows is no surprise. You have again been taught the lesson that you have steadfastly refused to remember.

Back in your car, you forage through the glovebox and console. You come up with a handful of change. You had intended to treat yourself to a nice brunch today. You use your credit card to purchase a bagel and coffee.

Interesting turn of events. "What is my fucking problem?"

You could have been working and billing your time. Surely you are "entitled" to some fun. Why does it have to be tied to gambling? Surely gambling is preferable to drugs or alcohol or sex. (What's the difference, pilgrim?)

Run silent, run deeper.

TRIAL DAY SIX

The jurors look none too pleased at the prospect of another week in the box. You have seen faces like this before. You think of those parents in Sunday clothing who drag their children door to door to spread the gospel of something or other. They ring the doorbells of impatiently polite homeowners. The look on the faces of those people being preached to want to scream, "Fuck off!" However, the presence of the prop children makes them an unwilling audience.

Lois is here. Schiff and the two assistants hover around her. She seems to enjoy the attention.

You flash to Norma Desmond in *Sunset Boulevard*: "I'm ready for my close-up, Mr. DeMille."

Lois is ready for hers.

Kate had planned to attend today. But she is not present. You are not surprised, and you are not sure if you are disappointed.

You have made plans with Adam to escort Laura to court today. But not until Lois is off the witness stand. You think that lovely, demure Laura, sitting quietly in the courtroom, will make a nice visual contrast with the angry Lois. You repeat your strict instructions to Adam and Laura: Do not make faces, nods, shakes of the head, or signs of emotion. Everything is noticed by jurors. Everything is magnified in trial.

Schiff is uncharacteristically solicitous and soft-spoken as he takes Lois through her testimony. Schiff is smart in having her appear almost last in his case. The jury already knows her story by virtue of it having been told by the prior witnesses, particularly Dr. Hector. All Lois has to do is look distraught and sob periodically. She does so. You realize that there is little to gain by keeping her on the stand and much to risk by looking like a bully. You conduct a cross-examination, which consists primarily of going through the list of healthcare providers she had seen in the past (impressively long). Then you let her go.

For the *pièce de résistance*, Schiff calls an economist to testify about the financial losses sustained by Ms. Sutcliffe due to Dr. Golden's misconduct. You have already heard all of this. You marvel at the straight face that this Stanford PhD keeps as he spins out calculations of the difference between Lois's earnings had she been a lawyer and the reality of her librarian wages. It turns out that she would have been pretty well-off. (Surprise, surprise!) You can't help thinking that you, on the other hand, might have been a lot better off financially if you had gone into library science instead of law. Making lots of money never equated to holding onto it for you.

Your cross-examination is exceedingly short. "Everything you have told us is dependent on Ms. Sutcliffe having told the truth about Dr. Golden, right?"

The economist supposes so. You turn to the gallery where Laura and Adam are seated.

You walk down the aisle and lean over, whispering in Laura's ear. "Just look thoughtful and nod."

As she does, you return to your seat and announce that you have no more questions. You are theatrical in your minimalist way. You want the jurors to connect all the talk about money damages to where it would come from: the nice widow. Schiff rests his case.

You and Manny exchange small talk in the hotel lobby. He asks whether you have been eating well during your stay. He has observed that you do not go out much at night and have sent out for a couple of pizzas. You reply that you are doing fine with a stash of PowerBars. Manny offers to bring you some of his wife's *pozole*. You pretend to know what that is but politely decline. You gaze in your bathroom mirror and try to assess whether the circles under your eyes are recent features. When the Mannys of the world are worried about your health, it may be time for a little lifestyle re-evaluation. (Nah. Down periscope.)

TRIAL DAY SEVEN

Your witnesses are lined up like torpedoes. You plan to fire them off in rapid succession. In addition to Dr. Golden's old friends, you had one real find: Dr. Kottke. He treated Lois for a few months when she first came to California. You had put him on your list of potential trial witnesses and had served him with a subpoena. But you had only met with him a week before trial. Schiff never took his deposition since you both had his rather brief and seemingly innocuous records regarding Lois.

Dr. Kottke remembers Lois well. It might be more accurate to say that he is still shaken by his experience with her 16 years ago. He was, at the time, a recently licensed physician who was starting a private psychiatry practice. Lois had been recently hospitalized after a suicide attempt and was referred to Dr. Kottke by a colleague at the hospital. Lois seemed to respond well to new antidepressants prescribed by Dr. Kottke. She also seemed very receptive to psychotherapy and attributed her improvement to Dr. Kottke's acumen. She sought to increase visits to two and even three times a week. Dr. Kottke consulted with a senior physician who cautioned against becoming "too enmeshed" with this patient's psychopathology. When Dr. Kottke told Lois that he would only be available for weekly appointments, she angrily terminated.

What Lois's records from Dr. Kottke did not show were the 10 to 15 subsequent phone calls made by Lois to his office and his home. She expressed her devastation at having been "deserted." She was the doctor's first "patient from hell." After Dr. Kottke enlisted an attorney to seek an injunction, Lois faded away.

Schiff is apoplectic. He has just been screwed by Dr. Kottke and you.

You have asked Laura to be present all day. Adam accompanies. You have told them about the importance of acting dignified and calm. Laura perfectly shows no reaction to the goings on. She is the picture of vulnerability and dignity. She is like English royalty without the arrogance. Every time you look at her, your heart breaks. You know that Schiff is chomping at the bit for his chance to tear into her on the witness stand.

You are pleased with yourself because you now know that is never going to happen. You have told Laura that tonight would be a perfect time for her to get away with David for a few days. You suggested some nice family resorts in Cabo San Lucas. By the time Schiff realizes that you are not calling Laura as a witness, she should be well out of subpoena range.

You present testimony from all of Dr. Golden's call group, with the exception of Dr. Witgang. As expected, they praise Dr. Golden and crap on Lois. Schiff does a good job of getting them to admit that they have no first-hand information as to what went on behind closed doors with Dr. Golden. They also grudgingly acknowledge that sexual exploitation by psychiatrists is a real phenomenon that does cause damage to patients.

Near the end of the day, you call Adam Golden. You previously provided him with the exact questions you would ask. As to cross-examination, you simply told Adam to tell the truth and not argue or express anger with Schiff. Most importantly, if Schiff asked what you had told Adam before taking the stand, he was to say that he had been instructed to be honest and to have faith in the jury's ability to not be fooled by Ms. Sutcliffe and her attorney. (You knew that this line of questioning was favored by Schiff with witnesses who were not parties and thus had no attorney-client privilege with you.)

After asking Adam some background questions, you get to the point. "Why do you want to be a doctor?"

"I was inspired by my father to devote my life to helping people."

"How much longer do you have to go in your training?"

"I will finish my coursework this year. Then I will have an internship, followed by a residency in which I plan on specializing in internal medicine. It should take another four years."

"During your training thus far, have you been taught about the importance of maintaining professional boundaries with your patients?"

"Absolutely. A doctor needs to respect the patient's confidentiality and keep the relationship focused on the problems for which the patient is being treated."

"Did you ever discuss that topic with your dad?"

"We had a long talk about that subject once"

"Tell us what was said."

Schiff jumps out of his chair and shouts, "Objection! Irrelevant!"

The judge gives Schiff the stank eye. "No. We want to hear the answer to that question."

You are pretty sure that this is the judge's way of paying Schiff back for having been such a tool throughout trial. You have a bunch of rationales to assert for the propriety of the question, had you been asked, but they are mostly bullshit.

Adam digs in. "I had been doing a student rotation through a hospital psychiatric unit. I found the patients interesting and began to talk about them at a Sunday brunch with the family. I gave details of their reasons for being hospitalized and told a story, which I thought was amusing, about a psychotic man who had been admitted after a dramatic standoff with the police. It was a matter that had made the local newspapers. I described the man's delusional rationales for his behavior.

"My dad cleared his throat and asked me to join him outside the restaurant. 'It is good that you are finding the work interesting. I know you have confidence that you can safely discuss your experiences with our family members. But you are violating the privacy of your patient. You have a sacred trust that you must not violate. First and foremost, do no harm. Don't talk about your patients except with other healthcare providers who are involved with their care. Show them the utmost respect.'

"We talked longer about the topics of boundaries and confidentiality. By the time we came inside, everyone had finished eating. Everyone knew that I had been taken to the woodshed. Nothing more was said."

"Adam, how long did you know your father?"

"Twenty-five years."

"Did you ever hear him talk about his clients?"

"No. He never did."

"Did you ever have any reason to believe that he did not keep strict professional boundaries with his patients?"

"No, sir."

You ask further questions about phone calls from Lois Sutcliffe after the death of Dr. Golden. Adam details his attempts to gently put Ms. Sutcliffe off, but ultimately he told her more directly to leave their family alone.

Schiff angrily dives in. "Mr.Golden, you can't say one way or another whether your father had sex with my client, can you?"

Adam pauses, then softly says, "Yes, sir. I can. It would be completely contrary to the man I knew for him to do such a thing."

Schiff jumps to his trump card. "How did your father meet his wife, Laura Golden?"

Your turn to object. "Your Honor, irrelevant and outside the scope of direct exam."

"Overruled."

Adam comes through with his understanding. "They had mutual friends who introduced them to each other. I guess you should ask Laura."

"Oh, I will. *Believe* me, I will." Schiff stomps back to his seat. "By the way, Mr. Golden, how much time did you spend with opposing counsel in preparation for your testimony today?"

Adam looks Schiff in the eye. "We met once. He told me to just tell the truth and to have faith in the judge and jury to do the right thing." (Score! Triple bonus points!)

Back in your hotel room, you order a pizza, call Miranda, and ask Manny for a bottle of Jack Daniels. The evening softly blurs.

TRIAL DAY EIGHT

You scrape white gunk off your tongue. You manage to avoid regurgitating the in-room coffee and a PowerBar. There is a swig of whiskey left in the bottle. Breakfast of Champions.

Today is an important trial day. You do not panic. Over the years, you have learned not to panic even when you assuredly should. Your two expert witnesses will testify today. They are both so accomplished and experienced in trial that you do not have to do much more than introduce them. In any event, you are fine. (Sure you are.)

Dr. Ussachevsky is a goddamn encyclopedia of psychology. He has committed to memory the thousands of pages of Lois Sutcliffe's treatment records. He has studied Dr. Witgang's detailed analysis of the fantasy relationship maintained by Lois in regard to Dr. Golden. Dr. Ussachevsky finds Witgang's notes to be "prescient." That is Ussachevsky's only downside. He is Russian born but somehow has an exceptional command of English vocabulary. (How does that happen?) You have to ask for a "translation" into layperson's language now and then.

"It is almost as if Dr. Witgang predicted with exquisite accuracy the path that Ms. Sutcliffe's pathology would take vis-à-vis Dr. Golden," says Dr. Ussachevsky.

By now, the jurors can probably recite from memory the DSM criteria for borderline personality disorder. You still have your blow up at hand, and Dr. Ussachevsky walks you through it. He gives specific examples from Sutcliffe's treatment records of each criterion:

- "Here are the multiple times she expressed her sense of being abandoned."

117

- "These are the unstable interpersonal relationships she has had, almost all of which alternated between love and hate."
- "Here are the instances in which she acknowledged instability in her sense of self."
- "These are the times she has engaged in selfdamaging impulsivity."
- "Her suicidal behavior has been manifest."
- "Here are her extremely reactive moods of depression, irritability, and anxiety."
- "She repeatedly has reported her feelings of emptiness."
- "She certainly is intensely and inappropriately angry on occasion."
- "She seems to have experienced paranoia in response to stress."

In short, the DSM diagnosis should be accompanied by Lois Sutcliffe's photograph. (Ussachevsky doesn't say that. But you think it and hope others are thinking it as well.)

Most importantly, Dr. Ussachevsky believes that a person with Lois's diagnosis and history would be particularly likely to react to the abandonment (by death) of a beloved psychotherapist with intense feelings and beliefs of betrayal.

Schiff goes after Dr. Ussachevsky. There are heated exchanges. It goes on for hours. At one point, Schiff insistently questions Dr. Ussachevsky regarding his relationship with you. Dr. Ussachevsky has testified for you in at least 10 other cases. You once invited him and his wife to a Super Bowl party. (This was when you were a domesticated person with a suburban wife and family.) Schiff suggests that Dr. Ussachevsky is biased by virtue of this event. He meticulously cross-examines Ussachevsky as to the menu for the party. (Schiff seems particularly interested in the selection of sliced meats.) You make no effort to object. You actually want to hear more about the party because your own recall is sketchy. The judge finally intervenes and instructs Schiff to "find something relevant to ask about."

On your scorecard, it is a clear TKO for Ussachevsky. However, you never get overconfident in trial. That is probably why you gild the lily by calling Dr. Martin as your next witness.

Dr. Martin has never met Lois Sutcliffe in person. You are presenting his expertise on the characteristics of people with borderline personality disorders. This is a sneaky technique of which you are particularly fond. Unfettered by the facts of a case, an expert can offer testimony of what people with certain diagnoses are known to think and do. The expert is immunized from cross-exam as to the facts of the case because he is only speaking in generalities and hypotheticals. Dr. Martin gives the equivalent of a seminar on borderline personality disorder. Such people cannot be "cured," only "managed." They frequently idolize their doctors but later believe the same people to be "monsters" who have ruined their lives. (Nuff said.)

Dr. Martin also takes exception to some of Dr. Hector's opinions. Schiff rails at Dr. Martin for his "audacity" in questioning the renowned Dr. Hector. No one else in the courtroom seems to be the least bit upset about this. Trial adjourns for the day.

After the jury files out, Schiff asks for your schedule of witnesses tomorrow. You tell him and the judge that you will not be calling any further witnesses but will only be offering some final exhibits into evidence. Schiff complains loudly that he has been led to believe that Laura Golden was going to testify.

You respond. "I considered it. Now I see no need. The defense will be resting tomorrow morning, Your Honor."

Schiff says that he will put on a rebuttal case. He will recall Dr. Hector and call Laura Golden himself. Good luck with that, you think. The judge issues an edict that everyone be ready to discuss jury instructions and do closing arguments tomorrow if time allows.

You call Adam and confirm that Laura has taken her vacation out of the country. You ask him to be ready to sit in court on Friday, symbolically representing "the family."

You return to the Sparta. You ask Manny to direct you to a good Mexican restaurant within walking distance. He talks you into taking a taxi to his brother's place a few miles away. Manny has called ahead, and you are treated like family. It would take a brave white man to venture into the Boca Longa alone without some positive recommendations. Several young men with low-rider trousers and dour expressions loiter outside. The broken fluorescent sign in the window reads, "Bo … Lo …"

Once through the thick double doors, another world beckons. The dining area is a large, well-lighted space with solid-wood tables and chairs. The darkened bar beckons seductively off to the side. You never make it there because the friendly waitress with a broad backside and a seductive smile brings *margarita* after *margarita* even though you have made no order.

"*No problema, chiquito*. Relax. You are *con amigos*."

You wonder if she has plans for later in the evening. It is purely theoretical. You are not going to be doing anything adventurous later this night, and you know it.

You eat (and enjoy) *pozole*. The *enchiladas camerones* are killer. The same can be said for the *margaritas*, which keep magically appearing. Other diners seem to be enjoying your presence. The feeling is mutual. You are blissfully zonked.

"Do you have room for some *sopapillas, Señor*?"

You are pretty sure that you do.

As you leave, you pause at the cashier's stand and thrust your hand into the large, plastic bowl, which is home to a thousand individually wrapped red-and-white striped mints. You enjoy the sensation a little too long and see the subtle looks of concern on your hosts' faces. You are bundled into a cab. Manny has to help you into your room. You thank him effusively for the best night of your San Jose stay. (Well, second best.) You have no idea how much cash you push into his hand.

TRIAL DAY NINE

D r. Hector is back for more. It seems a bit pathetic to you. Schiff informs the judge that his process servers have been unable to locate Laura Golden. He asks for a continuance of trial to allow her to be served.

"Denied."

Hector bores the heck out of everyone (you hope!) for a few more hours. You earn the gratitude of the jury (you hope!) by doing no cross-exam. The judge excuses the jury for the rest of the day. He efficiently and curtly goes through the jury instructions proposed by Schiff and you. Closing arguments will start first thing tomorrow.

You have outlined a comprehensive closing argument, but the night before delivering it is always fraught with second thoughts. Trial attorneys flatter themselves to think that their oratory skills have significant impact on what a jury decides. Scientific studies continually establish that jurors have made up their minds well before the attorneys argue at the end of trial. But you guys like it. It is the only time that you can directly tell the jury what you think they ought to do. You give your pages a lot of second thought.

You suck and chew deliberately on the red-and-white mints that you find on the nightstand. You decide to go commando — at least as far as words are concerned.

CLOSING ARGUMENT

Schiff addresses the jury. He is in fine form. You are not closely listening to what he says. But he certainly cuts an imposing figure. His tailored suit is better than anything in your closet. His shoes are shined to a high gloss. (Oops, you forgot about that.) You are pretty sure that he gets manicures. The two assistants are gazing at him like Nancy Reagan used to beam at Ronald. Two hours into his closing argument, he has not yet hit the floor. You are not sure whether that is a good or bad omen.

It will be your turn soon. You will say your words. You have a legal pad full of them. You decide to stick with last night's inspiration. You suddenly realize that everyone is staring at you. You have been lost in thought. (But likely just look lost.) The judge is glowering. You feel the tension in the courtroom.

You get on your feet and head for the lecture stand. "I never met Dr. Golden. Nor did any of you. But after this trial, I feel that I know him rather well. And I think you do too. We have also come to know Lois Sutcliffe. You may have sympathy for her unhappy life. Dr. Golden certainly did. But sympathy is not a substitute for justice. It's just not.

"I have to admit that I did not listen all that attentively to everything Mr. Schiff said in his long speech. But I did hear him say that his client's testimony was uncontradicted by any evidence. That is not so. Ms. Sutcliffe's allegations are contradicted by everything we have learned about Dr. Golden's professional practice and his life. They are contradicted by what we know about Ms. Sutcliffe's mental disorder. Mr. Schiff also said something about my having hid from you the testimony of Dr. Golden's wife. I am hopeful that you share with me the view that Dr. Golden's wife has been put through quite enough.

"I know that you will do your best to follow the judge's instructions as to how you should deliberate. On behalf of Dr. Golden's family. For Dr. Golden, my client, I thank you for your time and attention." You have just gone out on a fragile limb. You have invested in the idea that short is truly sweet. People who pay your bills tend to expect more of an effort in a closing argument. The insurance company's representative is looking at you as if she wishes she had an automatic weapon. Words. Maybe you did not employ enough of them. Now you wait.

BASKING IN THE GLORY

The Sutcliffe jury has done its job. The court clerk smiles at you. The bailiff shakes your hand. The jurors are waiting in the hall to chat. You try to mask your impatience as people earnestly seek to inform you about the details of deliberations and to compliment you on the way you have fought for truth and justice. You don't have much curiosity about their group's thought processes nor do you invest very much in their admiration. You know that it is all a crap shoot. But it is fun to win at craps. You prefer it to the alternative.

As it turns out, you were wrong — as usual — about most of your juror assessments. The foreperson was the guy you thought was a stoner. The jury had split 11 to one. The one who wanted to find in favor of Lois Sutcliffe was your ex-wife substitute. (No surprise there.)

The next day, you return phone messages that have accumulated over the course of this trial. One is from your attorney friend Brian Donnelly. He invites you to lunch, an event that you simultaneously look forward to and dread. The positive anticipation is because Brian is a great attorney and storyteller. He enlightens you on odd legal issues and makes you laugh. The dread is because you know that you will drink excessively, blow off the rest of the afternoon, and have a brain-splitting headache the following day. You spend a few moments on the horns of that dilemma before returning the call and making a date. Brian tells you of an upcoming appellate hearing in which he hopes to put an end to a long and tedious lawsuit.

"It sounds like a winner to me, Brian," you offer.

"From your lips to God's ears," he replies.

"What's that about lips?"

"It's an old Irish expression. My people are prone to the invocation of divine interest in our mundane human affairs."

You vaguely recall something, the significance of which is dim.

Almost immediately after hanging up the phone, you get a call from Adam Golden. He is grateful for your hard work. "You sure put that disgusting blackmailer in her place!"

Because it is a topic about which you have strong feelings, you respond pedantically. "Sutcliffe wasn't technically a blackmailer. She didn't try to secretly extort money from anyone. She filed a lawsuit, which — misguided as it was — was subject to a fair fight in a court of law."

Adam is silent on the other end of the line. He is quiet a little too long for comfort. Finally, he says, "Well, thanks so much anyway. It means a lot to the whole family." Click.

You have a funny feeling. Did Lois ever try to blackmail someone? Of course, she never would have admitted doing so. Did the family keep something from you? Does that matter? Why don't you just turn your brain off for a while? But you can't quite shut it down. There has always been something a bit fishy about Laura, Adam, and ... Dr. Witgang! What did he say about Lucas's last words? How did he know that Laura was on Dr. Golden's lips as he died? And what could that mean?

You know better than to continue this line of thought. But that afternoon you call Kate and ask her to get you a copy of Dr. Golden's death certificate. That evening, you drink a bottle of Pouilly-Fuissé and go to sleep.

When you awake, it is a bright, crisp fall day, full of promise and new beginnings. There is a lightness in your step as you bounce into the office. You are ready to receive the congratulations of your peers, who should be calling over the next few days.

On your chair is a copy of Golden's death certificate. There it is. The signature of the attending physician, attesting to the cause of death by cardiac arrest: Marcus Witgang, MD. Witnessed by Adam Golden. (How cozy.)

DONE WITH THE WIDOW

You get on the phone and make two appointments for the following day: Dr. Witgang and Laura Golden. Kate asks to talk. The hair on your neck stands up. Kate gives her two-week notice. She is going to take a part-time job at a large defense firm. She is also enrolling in a law school with an evening program. You look in her eyes. They are vacant. The connection between the two of you has been ruptured. You feel like a douchebag. You congratulate her and wish her well.

You try to look composed as you slink out of your office and past Lawrence, who is sitting at his desk. He makes no eye contact, which is the Lawrence equivalent of shouting, "You dirty bastard!" Even when he periodically holds you in contempt, he has something caustic to say and always gives you one of the "looks worth a thousand words."

You get it. Not only have you wrecked a fun and efficient working relationship with your legal assistant, you have ruined the best part of Lawrence's work days. You wonder if you will lose him soon too. (Would an impromptu salary increase be too obvious an act of desperate insecurity?)

You feel guilty and anticipatorily lonely. You must look blatantly lost because, after a while, Lawrence takes pity and speaks. "Erections are known to divert blood flow from the brain. I forgive you, dummy."

You almost — but not quite — shed a tear. You have an urge to hug the chubby fellow. But that might start something in an entirely wrong direction.

You pose nonchalantly in Kate's doorway. "I never asked if there was anything I can do to make you reconsider staying here."

"No. You didn't." Kate is icy.

"Maybe you could do your part-time work here while you go to law school. It could be as flexible as you need for study time. Or maybe you could take a six-month sabbatical, with some pay, to think things over. Or maybe I could finally set up that employee 401(k). Or maybe I could just stand on my head and beg you not to go."

Kate looks at you and smiles. "Stop. If there is one thing you have taught me from your law practice and your several marriages, it is this: Between men and women, timing is everything. We have had our time together. Let's not mess up the great memories by trying to force them into the future."

Since she is now smiling, you break out a pseudo-grin of your own. Kate gives you a fierce hug. You know that this hug will have to keep you for a long while. You know that your failure to maintain "boundaries" is to blame for your feeling of desertion. You meditate on the paradoxical relationship between intention and outcome. You go for a walk. You drink some beer. You sleep fitfully and are up early. You look like shit.

Next day, you are off to see Dr. Witgang. Old Dr. Meerschaum Tweedy Coat knows that something is up but welcomes you into his office as though you were a dear friend. His eyes give him away. They dart from side to side and never quite meet yours. The cherry tobacco smells rotten.

"Doctor, you did a good job of pretending to be Lucas Golden's friend and admirer. I bought it. When the shit comes down, I sure hope that Adam and Laura don't turn on you." (You are improvising.)

The caring health professional is curious. "I have no idea what you are talking about. Are you ill?"

"You were there when Golden died. You told me his last words. You signed his death certificate. You were helping Laura resolve a sticky situation. You knew that Lois was extorting money from Lucas. You knew everything. That's why you talked me out of calling you as a witness. You would have had to tell too many lies."

Witgang puckers his mouth as though he has tasted something bitter. "You know whatever you know. Trial is done. Lucas is gone. Life goes on. Why don't you do the same?" He stands up and opens the office door.

You drive to Laura Golden's house. She meets you at the door and immediately dispels all notions of cat and mouse. You are both cats. The cornflower-blue eyes are not quite as clear as you remembered them. There is something a little hard around the corners that you had not previously noticed.

"Marcus called a few minutes ago. He says that you have figured some things out. Good for you. Better late than never. I don't think there is anything you can do about it. I have been advised that you and I have an attorney-client privilege. I am sure that you would not want to go through the kind of ethics complaint process and legal actions that my family could muster if needed. Plus, I like you and think you care about me too. We can certainly work out some kind of arrangement going forward." (Is she talking money? Sex? Something else? How about answers?)

"Did Lois Sutcliffe demand money from Lucas before he died?"

"She wanted $2 million. Lucas was willing to pay it. He could. It would, however, have resulted in selling our home and drastically cutting back on our expenses. Why would I ever allow that?"

"You're saying that your husband did in fact have a sexual relationship with Lois?"

"He fucked her. He fucked us all. That is the kind of doctor he was."

"You and Adam put him out of business?"

"You could put it that way."

"Why did Dr. Witgang help out?"

"That old gasbag was the one who transferred me to the loving care of Dr. Golden." Her voice is thick with sarcasm. "He was sick of covering up for his so-called friend. Who knows? Maybe he thought that he would get a shot at me once Lucas was gone. He didn't do any of the heavy lifting anyway. Just helped with the legal documents after the fact."

"If that is true, how did he know Lucas's last word, which was supposedly your name?"

"I suppose that Lucas was not *technically* deceased by the time Witgang arrived at the house. If he had something to say about me by that time, I'm sure it wasn't too complimentary." Laura is actually smirking. She must have carried hate in her heart for a very long time. Or maybe she is another example of your inability to quickly spot psychopathology in clients. "I am still young. I have a chance at a new life with Adam and my son. Why not accept that sometimes drastic remedies need to be employed? You helped us, and I will always be grateful. Let's be friends. *Good* friends." Laura leans closer. You feel her breath on your face. You momentarily enjoy the sensation of unrequited sin.

You pride yourself on being a realist. As a general rule, people are not better than you thought they were. If anything, they turn out to be worse. Nevertheless, you usually think the best of people until proven wrong. And then you are proved wrong.

You are trying to speak in a measured tone and a calm pace. "I don't care about the death of Lucas Golden. He must have been a prick. I don't care that you and Adam apparently killed him. I truly don't give a fuck. It was understandable. Maybe the right thing to do, all things considered. But what I *do* care about — what pisses me off — is that you used me. I threw myself into this case, defending the good name and reputation of someone who did not warrant my efforts. I don't know if I care as much about what you did to your husband as I do about the fact that you all played me. Either way, I'm keeping my distance. Don't write. Don't call. Don't send a Christmas card. I sure as hell won't be giving you a thought. Goodbye, Mrs. Golden."

You are unsteady as you traverse the manicured front lawn and enter your car.

Can you really put Laura and your now-empty victory out of your mind? You used to be the kind of person who could do so. You have buried and locked away far more than your share of neuronal synapses — especially those carrying your own misdeeds and embarrassments. For some reason, this feels like an experience that will stick.

At the moment, you need some inhibitory adjustment. You will go with gin and tonic. As you have many times since you were eight years old, you fantasize about running away to join the circus. The gin begins to slowly dilate the blood vessels, feeding the nerves in your corpus callosum, where the halves of your brain join to compare notes. As the connections cross, you recall that you figuratively made that mad dash years ago. You can't drink enough to forget the identity of the clown.

DAYS LIKE THIS

You hear something. Consciousness is taking its time. An unpleasant noise is coming from your cell phone, which is lying on the floor in a corner of your room. Your ring tone is "Welcome to the Working Week" by Elvis Costello. You are awake enough to hate the irony, which you once thought clever.

Lawrence is calling to report that your 9 a.m. appointment has left in a huff.

"What time is it anyway?" you inquire groggily.

"Ten thirty. Bad night?"

"How the hell would *I* know?" (You actually don't.)

"Should I send paramedics?"

"I'll be there in a while. Anything else that I've screwed up?"

"You got a certified letter from the IRS."

"You didn't sign for it, did you?"

"You know me better than that, boss."

"You are a good person, Lawrence."

"Well, that and $3.95 will get me a Starbucks cappuccino."

"You are very philosophical too. 10-4."

Your standard ablutions (teeth brushing, shaving, showering) take twice as long as usual. Your head is painful and large. You cannot remember the means by which you got home last night nor the actions leading to your bed. You can't find your car keys. You call a cab. Checking your wallet, you find sufficient cash for the cab and the $3.95 Starbucks beverage referred to by Lawrence. You have the driver drop you halfway between work and coffee, reasoning that you are exercising by virtue of walking a total of six blocks.

You question the rationale for everything you do. You feel empty. No Kate. No Laura. What is the point of the continuing struggle?

An old African American man paces outside Starbucks. He has the requisite grocery-store shopping cart full of raggedy garbage nearby. He looks like an experienced panhandler. He calmly sizes up approaching pedestrians and seems to select only the most likely donors for purposes of delivering his plea.

"Any little bit will help! I am down on my luck. But I'm not giving up. Give a man a helping hand! Please, sir. Open up your heart!"

The old man waves a torn piece of cardboard on which is written, "Mama said there'd be days like this. No money. No food. No shelter."

You confront the panhandler. "Whose song was that?"

"It's mine."

"No. I mean who did the song, 'Mama Said (There'd Be Days Like This)?'"

He looks peeved. "It's my sign!"

"I *know* it is your sign. There was a song with that lyric. I want to know who performed it."

"It's my song!"

You stare at each other for a few seconds. There is no way to bridge the gap.

"It's my song too, brother," you mumble. You hand him your last $5 bill.

Better late than never, a new day has begun.

ABOUT THE AUTHOR

John Fleer, PhD, JD, has been a litigation attorney for 37 years. He lives in northern California with his wife Marika and five cats.

Made in the USA
Columbia, SC
03 December 2018